COUNT EVERY STAR

NANCY ELVIRA

Copyright © 2014 Nancy Elvira
ISBN 978-0-692-29362-1

Cover Design by Julie D. Womack

Cover Photographs
"Night on the Town" ©Nancy Womack

Young Couple in Love Outdoor ©
Arthur Hidden - Thinkstock

Manufactured in the United States of America

To the city of Cleveland, Ohio,
and
her colorful, everyday cast of characters.

Count Every Star

Haunting sirens, wailing in the distance, were rapidly becoming overshadowed by flashing lights gaining intensity in the foreground.

A roadblock of first responders' vehicles skewed across the Edgewater entrance was the first clue that something was very wrong. Strobes blazed everywhere, in blinding shades of red and blue, providing stiff competition for the city lights reflecting off the lake.

That was the second clue.

The untamed energy of a curious crowd, overloaded the night air, making it difficult to breathe. An unattended ambulance waited by the side of the road as frustrated police officers struggled to restrain aggressive, curious onlookers.

Beyond the bend, directly above the homes on the ridge, the night sky glowed with an ominous, eerie radiance.

Headlights rounded the corner, growing larger as a car approached, barely skidding to a stop before the driver's door flew open.

A distraught young woman vaulted from the vehicle, slipping on the icy street as she fought through the crowd, desperately trying to break through the roadblock. She was first ignored, and then held back by the police. She protested, jerking against the unrelenting grip on her arms.

"Please ... God, Please! My grandmother's house is up there! Let me through!!" Cold wind whistled through the air, chapping her cheeks.

Heartbroken and helpless, tears streaming down her face, she fixed her stare up at the horizon. She gulped, the realization sinking in that her hopes, dreams and memories were most likely being reduced to a mere pile of flickering embers.

~ ONE ~

ALEX DASHED QUICKLY out the door, ducking under low hanging tree branches as he made his way to the street.

Ironically, dodging the icy limbs that obscured his view was symbolic of his outlook on life in Cleveland Ohio, in general. There was always something in the way; something preventing him from getting exactly what he wanted.

It didn't take a genius to figure out that only one person had gone in to the office that day. The beam on the pole spotlighting the vintage, red 1967 Mustang underlined that fact.

Wagner; Alex Wagner.

That would not have surprised anyone at Oz Communications. Alex was one of those guys who defined the word "workaholic."

If he had been daydreaming, Alex would have been rudely startled back to consciousness as his foot stepped off the curb ... right into a deep pothole in the street, cleverly disguised by a deceivingly solid crust of snow. The slush slithered up past his shoe, through his sock and gripped his ankle. He recoiled in shock.

The string of profanity that fell from his lips would have made a WWII sailor blush. He quickly withdrew his foot, but the damage had already been done.

A semi-frozen slurry of slush whipped against his face with a passing car. Alex cringed; the bitter chill of winter encircled him again, strongly suggesting he pull the collar of his jacket higher up around his neck.

He shivered as he approached the car while speaking into his phone. "Damn, it's cold! January can't get here soon enough!"

"Yeah, I was the only one working today." He watched his breath transform into puffy smoke signals and he continued to speak. "Look - *I know* it's the day after Thanksgiving. You know how I feel about holidays."

Alex grumbled as he paused briefly to unlock the car. "I'm on my way - see you in about ten." He made a face, jumped into the car quickly, shifted the old ragtop into gear and headed for the exit.

Holiday salutations threatened his very existence, relentlessly nagging at him, reminding him that Christmas was only a month away.

As if he could forget it. Everywhere he went he found himself bombarded with an endless barrage of festive music, lighted displays and euphoric merriment. There was no escape.

It wasn't that he hated the Christmas season; he just wished it only went on for about 2 days. Then life could just return to normal.

About as normal as life could ever be for Alex Wagner.

He peeled off the wet gloves with his teeth and tossed them on the passenger seat while concentrating on a vision of the brew that would be waiting at the table for him. The anticipation had him so focused that he was unaware of the fact that his front right tire had rolled over a nail in the parking lot as he made his departure.

Alex was trapped in heavy rush-hour traffic before he began to sense that the car was having a problem, but he didn't know what it was yet. He eventually became painfully aware that the tire was going flat by the uneven roll of his vehicle, flip-flopping as he began to slow down.

He pulled off the freeway at the next exit ramp and into the safe haven of the first parking lot he saw. Overcome with a feeling of absolute disgust, he walked around the car, squeezing his hands back into the dripping wet gloves; he shuddered and removed the spare tire from the trunk. Alex drew a breath and shook his head: he was thoroughly irritated.

"Shit! That's just *great!*" As he dodged in and out of the mixed concoction of precipitation, he tightened the grip his scarf had around his neck and began the painful process of changing the tire.

Lights from the large chain of cars on the freeway sparkled on the horizon behind him as he tightened the last of the bolts and stood.

Sleet, slush, *shlit*; Alex never did know exactly what to call it. Whatever it was, he did not appreciate it in the least. Alex hoisted the old tire into the trunk and slammed the lid. He removed his gloves again.

Something at the edge of his vision caught his attention as he hastily dove back into the car and hit the ignition. Alex breathed life back into his icy, clasped fingers and slowly turned his head, when his eyes finally settled on a towering, red brick building. On the other side of the building, tucked behind the trees, was a paved playground.

A momentary rush came over Alex as he realized he was looking at the old school he had attended as a child. The aged wrought iron bench he remembered was still there. It had been painted a different color, but it was the same bench. Mulling over how long it had been since he'd been on that playground, his eyes were drawn to a door at the side of the school.

The darkness of the night parted, escorting him back to the memory of one recess in particular:

10-year-old Alex is in his room, talking on the telephone with one of his friends from school. He is secretly working on creating something while talking. Alex asks his friend,

"... you know that girl we saw today at recess; the one with the smile?"

"How am I supposed to know who she is? She's just some girl with glasses!" he answers, uninterestedly. Quickly changing the subject, his voice trails off and the phone conversation ends.

Alex is sitting at his desk, diligently creating an elaborate valentine, using everything from watercolors and markers to stickers and crayons. His finishing touch is a large heart-shaped sticker that reads,

"Be My Valentine." On the next line, double-coated in red and gold glitter is the word:

"Forever."

He smiles, pleased with the finished product. Alex searches his pencil jar for "just the right pen" to sign it with. Covering his signature with his hand, "just in case somebody is watching," he signs his masterpiece.

Alex places the valentine in an over-sized red envelope that clearly is not meant for this card. He seals it and tucks it inside his jacket, hanging it on the hook behind his door.

Alex's recollection moved on to the following day:

On the playground, 10-year-old Alex spots the awkwardly cute girl by the bench. He walks nervously in her direction. Although she is engrossed in conversation with another girl, she senses he is looking in her direction from across the yard.

Alex approaches; she leans to the right and watches him walking toward her. Her friend is called away, leaving her standing next to the bench alone. Alex's ten-year-old heart races with each step.

Suddenly, the warning bell rings to signal the end of recess. The playground becomes an unruly collection of chaotic juveniles, scrambling to get to their respective lines at one of the two doors before the tardy bell sounds.

He still has time. He keeps walking. Alex is about 10 feet from her, when his buddies playfully sweep him up in a wave of 10-year-old boys, racing to see who can get to the entrance first. Alex quickly hides the envelope under his jacket as the second and final bell sounds.

As Alex flees to the far door at the other end of the building, the envelope falls out of his jacket and onto the playground.

Moments later, Alex waits until his classmates have hung their jackets on the hooks. He quickly pats his jacket with both hands, searching for the envelope. Feeling nothing, he frantically sheds the jacket and shakes it -- no card.

Visibly distracted by the missing valentine, he hangs his jacket on the hook and takes his seat at his desk. The sound of the teacher's voice begins the afternoon lesson.

Alex frowned as he strained to recall more of the incident. He blinked his eyes, squeezed them shut for a second, and then quickly opened them again, dragging his brain back to the present. He shook his head.

Damn holidays. Nothing more than a shameless ploy to get people to spend money. What a complete waste of time!

He shifted the car in gear, rejoining the string of glistening taillights back onto the freeway.

~ TWO ~

HIS FRIENDS WERE ALREADY sitting at the table when Alex entered the pub. Eternally grateful for the beer waiting for him in front of the empty chair, he hesitated for a moment, stomping his feet on the mat, brushed off the loose snowflakes and walked toward the table. Alex threw his jacket on the chair, parked himself and sighed.

"Thanks. I've been waiting all afternoon for this." He threw back the mug and reduced its contents by about half. He exhaled. "Winter in Cleveland ... It can kiss my sorry ass!"

Alex's friend, Mike, leaned toward him slightly and whispered, "Hey, there's somebody you have got to meet." He discreetly pointed toward a table of women, across the crowded room.

Alex turned his head slightly. Considering that most of the women at the table were relatively attractive, he smirked. "Which one?"

There was one woman at the table that stood apart from the others. Her eyes flashed at Alex. Mike stood and motioned for her to come over. With her glass in hand, she stood. Flawless and dripping with self-confidence, she took her time, but she eventually arrived at Alex's table.

Mike placed an arm around her shoulders. "Alex, this is my wife's cousin, Claire. I couldn't believe it when I saw her walk in tonight."

Mike grinned at her. "Can you join us?"

Claire glanced back at her table. "... I suppose I could. I can't leave for long; it's a retirement party for one of my people."

Alex took note that it was an odd way of putting it, but he shrugged the comment off as he gave her the once-over and pulled out a chair. "... at least for a couple minutes?"

Claire plopped down, wasting no time as she scooted her chair closer to Alex. If she had gotten any closer, she would have been in his lap.

The waitress brought her another glass of wine. After a quick sip, Claire further introduced herself to Alex as he felt her shoeless foot rubbing against one of his calves, under the table. They locked eyes and she moved her foot upward. She rested her glass on the table in front of her and gave him a self-assured smile. The corners of his mouth turned upward slightly too, as he realized Claire's actions were not accidental.

"So ... you're Suzanne's cousin?"

"I lived on the same street as to Suzanne for about ten years, but when my father moved us out to the suburbs, I became a transplant." She laughed. "That is, until I moved my business downtown."

Mike placed his hand on the back of her chair and explained, "Claire has her own ad agency."

But before he could say anything else, a cake was whisked out to the table with Claire's friends. Clearly annoyed at the inconvenience, she excused herself. "I really should be over there right now."

Alex nodded in agreement. "Absolutely. Hey - any chance you'll be here *next* Friday?"

Claire squeezed past him, deliberately allowing her body to linger just long enough to serve as a tease. A spark flew as her eyes flashed again at Alex. She leaned in and whispered in an unmistakable tone,

"Anything's possible." And she went back to her table.

Mike dramatically fanned himself as she walked away. "Why the hell does every hot woman you meet want to mount you, instantly?"

Alex shot Mike a smug grin and picked up his mug. And they both enjoyed the view as they watched Claire continue to her table.

The two celebrations continued, independently, Claire catching Alex's eye from across the crowded room, every chance she got.

~ THREE ~

ALEX STEPPED OUT ONTO the landing of the converted old brownstone condominium on Clifton Road.

A light from a post above shone on the street in front of him as if to be pointing the way. His breath announced its presence in the form of a grayish-white vapor, rising into the Cleveland heavens overhead as a city snowplow passed him by.

He glanced upward. Snowflakes flirted with the sky, warning of a blizzard in the making but, by his calculations and vast experience with Cleveland weather, he still had time. He headed down the steps and hung a right when he reached the sidewalk.

~ ~ ~ ~ ~

She skidded down the uneven slope, icy branches lashing at her face while she clutched at shadowy objects, clawing for something solid to grasp.

Her head banged a rock and she came to a stop. Listening to the sounds of the lake, lapping against the shore, she clung there for a minute and breathed in a sigh of relief. She shifted her weight a little, until she was finally able to grab hold of a branch and pull herself into a sitting position.

Her arms were tired; her shoulders ached from the strain. She eyed her shadowy surroundings – and she felt like crying.

~ ~ ~ ~ ~

Alex ran along the lighted road, veering slightly to the left, toward the lakefront. As the sign for the park passed him by, his peripheral sent him a signal; the familiar Cleveland skyline crept into view, all aglow, looking exceptionally striking and compelling. He found it impossible to resist.

After hesitating for only a moment, he backtracked and decided to take the alternate path to take in the city lights. When he reached the fork in the road, he peeled off in the direction of the marina and the park along the icy water's edge. But he soon found himself losing momentum when his eyes shifted to the cliff face ahead.

He could make out the obscure silhouette of a man standing on a narrow piece of ground in between the treacherous, rocky overhang and the road. He laughed a little to himself at that.

God must have skipped that guy when he was passing out brains.

All of a sudden, the figure slipped silently into the shadows, and dropped off Alex's radar completely. He scanned the cliff one more time to see if he could locate the man. No such luck.

What else could he do?

While mumbling to himself about how unbelievably irresponsible some people can be, he quickly altered his route and ran the upward way onto Edgecliff Drive.

Edgecliff was only a one-sided strip of winding road stitched along the shoreline of Lake Erie, but it was a scenic route and it did make for an enjoyable run when he remembered to go that way.

By the time Alex got there, he was almost completely out of breath. He stopped to investigate.

Alex peered over the edge, past the guardrail. He was surprised to see a young woman sitting in the snow, hanging onto the cliff edge. He shouted down the bank,

"You okay?"

She heard something from the street above her. The frightened woman glanced up at Alex. With a relieved look in her eyes, she answered him.

"I'm fine." She laughed, nervously. "I guess I went a little too far."

That's an understatement.

Alex climbed over the guardrail. Debris began to roll toward her, as he moved down the hill. He skidded down the steep decline and landed on his behind. He quickly recovered and then sidestepped carefully down the narrow bank to the woman. Alex stretched his hand toward her.

"Here, take my hand."

The woman gratefully reached up and Alex pulled her to her feet, without slipping. Keeping a firm grip on her hand, he helped her navigate the treacherous terrain safely uphill and assisted her back over the guardrail to the street. Alex stared back at the barrier and the rocky cliff that lay beyond it.

"You know, that's why they're called guardrails."

"I know," she answered him sheepishly, brushing off the loose snow. Then, leaning on the fence, she continued, "I'm just not used to all these changes."

Alex began running in place. "Are you from around here?"

She gazed out over the lake and skyline. Then she turned and pointed to a big, sprawling, multi-level bungalow, across from the point. "My grandparents' house is right over there."

In a voice filled with whimsy, she added, "Well, it *used* to be their home." She returned her gaze back to the Cleveland skyline, across the lake. "It's sort of *my* house, I guess - at least for a couple of weeks anyway." She approached the driveway.

Alex followed alongside the woman, still running in place.

"My grandmother is not doing well. I don't know how much longer she has." She fumbled with the buttons on her jacket. "She was getting along fairly well on her own before she got sick. I had to move her to an assisted living facility about a month ago. Now, they're telling me to start thinking about hospice." She turned into the circular drive leading to the house. "She gave me the house and she wants me to sell it."

Alex was intrigued by the old place; he wondered what it looked like on the inside.

"I came in this afternoon from New York for a few weeks - just long enough to clean everything out and get the house ready to be put on the market." She continued up the driveway of the house with Alex in tow.

His dark brows drew together over his eyes. He asked, "And your grandfather?"

"He's been gone almost 20 years. Heart attack. I was only eleven." She hesitated at the front door; she appeared deep in thought. "My grandmother was so lost." She let out a sigh and gazed up at the dark windows of the upper floor of the building, then to the empty front of the entire house.

"It used to be so full of life … and love."

Alex gave up on running in place. "She never remarried? … Your grandmother, I mean."

She rolled her eyes slightly and smiled, polishing a handcrafted firefighter-emblem knocker with her gloved hand. "I don't think the thought ever crossed her mind." She shook her head and laughed.

"Grandfather had a mind of his own. He joined the Navy right out of high school when he was only 17. Then, a week before he was shipping out, he met *Irene*. They almost didn't get married but, *through a series of events*, as my grandfather used to say, they found each other again."

Her mouth shut with a snap as she caught herself rambling to this man she just met, and she suddenly stopped talking. "Oh, listen to me. I'm sorry to go on and on." She rolled her eyes.

"So what got them back together?"

"They both had this little saying: *missed opportunities will find their way back to you, if they are meant to be.* She bit her bottom lip. "Oh, there I go again!" She retracted the keys from her jacket pocket, and then she smiled up at Alex.

"I can't believe I haven't even thanked you for rescuing me from a slippery winter swim in the lake." She removed her right glove and offered her hand. "I'm Sarah."

Alex laughed and took her hand.

Sarah felt a sudden stirring of excitement. It completely defied logic, but her blood pressure shot up so high she could actually hear it rushing in her ears.

"Hi Sarah. I'm Alex." He began running in place again.

"Maybe we'll bump into each other again, before you leave. I usually run in this neighborhood."

"I hope so. Good night, Alex." She offered up an ear-to ear grin. "You know, I feel like I have just made my first friend in Cleveland."

Sarah stepped into the house. The door closed behind her. Alex watched as the light in the window turned on.

And he continued on his run.

~ FOUR ~

ALEX CARRIED A BOWL of popcorn to the couch and he sank into the soft cushions in front of the television. The local weather report brought a cringe to his face.

"Brace yourselves, Cleveland, for the first blizzard of the season."

He quickly grabbed the remote changing the station, only to find another weather forecast. "Expect anywhere between 4 to 6 inches of the white stuff by morning."

Shit.

Alex grabbed the remote again, desperately giving it one last try for something better, but was joined by another local meteorologist, who he had been watching on TV since *the beginning of time;* the 1980's. The recognition evoked a slight upward turn at the corners of Alex's mouth.

The kind, grandfatherly-looking man smiled and stared straight at the camera, but it looked to Alex like he was addressing him personally. "Folks, it looks like winter is back, and with a vengeance. You can expect anywhere from 4 to 8 inches of snow by the morning, depending on where you live."

Alex fell back down, hard, on the sofa cushion. He seized a pillow from the couch and covered his head to muffle the sound of the soothing television voice. He breathed deeply, closed his eyes and drifted off.

Alex's twitching and facial expressions reflected those of one who was having a nightmare. He tossed and winced anxiously as the TV weather special continued in the background. Vivid reminders of what it was like to fight the freezing temperatures seeped in, along with endless streams of ice and snow, slithered into his sleep.

But his delusions were rudely interrupted by the ringer on his cell phone. Half asleep, Alex slid off the couch onto the floor, popcorn bowl following, hurling popcorn all across the room. He jumped up, wild-eyed, as if he had just awakened from a bad, bad dream. Disoriented, he staggered over to his phone.

"Uh, hello?"

Frank, Alex's older brother, apologized. "Oh, sorry man. Were you asleep?"

Alex paused to gather his thoughts while he assembled stray popcorn strewn all over his living room. "I must have dozed off. I'm glad you woke me up. I had the weirdest nightmare."

"Hey - when did you say your last day in town was again?"

Alex answered in a tone infused with pure excitement. "I have exactly five days to find a place to live and get back here to finalize the transfer. I can drive through the night if I leave late on the 22nd, and stay through Christmas. I should be back on the 27th."

He continued collecting popcorn off the floor. "If everything goes as planned, I'll be out of here for good the week after New Year's." He was elated.

But Frank responded in a tone steeped with exasperation. "And, *of course* you have it planned - all on a strict schedule, with no room for change!" He huffed in frustration. "Talk about a completely rigid, unbendable guy!"

After a slight pause, he realigned his ammunition and asked, "Why do you always have to be so *anal-retentive?* What are you afraid of? I don't know why you can't open your new business here - instead of going so far away!"

"No way! That'll **never** happen. There's *nothing* for me in Cleveland!" A deafening silence followed.

"Ouch -- Alex, did I really screw you up *that* bad?"

"You?" Alex wheezed. "I'm the one that screwed *your* life up!" He stood and looked out the window to the traffic driving by and continued. "When all your friends were away at school, and living the good life, you had to stay home with *me*."

Frank raised his voice. "You know that was by choice, Alex. *Nothing* was more important to me than to raise you like mom and dad raised me. They loved you. They would be so proud of you. Mom really used to worry about you, you know." He inhaled deeply and huffed out.

"And what makes you think I'm **not** *living the good life* now?" Frank's voice softened. "Alex - when are you going to stop blaming yourself for my late start? After all, I never would have met Robyn -- and Gracie and Tyler wouldn't be a part of my life either, if I had settled with someone else sooner. I have a job I love, good friends … What more could I want?"

Then, after a slight hesitation, he went on. "I should be *thanking* you, Alex!"

An uneasy silence followed.

Alex changed the subject. "Well, the weather does factor heavily into my decision. You know I hate the frigid winters here."

"I think we both need to get some sleep," Frank said, in an apologetic tone. "Call me tomorrow, Ok?"

Alex finished dumping the last of the popcorn in the trash can on his way to the refrigerator. He took out a carton of milk and drank from the container, then he put the carton back in the fridge and closed the door. "Ok, buddy. Love you."

Alex turned out the floor lamp in the living room, and wandered down the hall to the bedroom. He flipped on the light from the wall switch at the door. Pulling back the covers, he climbed into bed.

But as he reached over to turn off the lamp, he hesitated instead and picked up the picture of his parents on the nightstand. He closed his eyes and tried to picture his mom and dad.

Even though his memories were mostly good ones, he had blocked a lot of them out to the point where he only remembered bits and pieces.

Alex knew, deep in his heart, that it wasn't his fault that his parents had been on the freeway that fateful night so many years ago. His biggest regret was that he had fought with them – like all 12-year-old kids do with their parents.

And that he had refused to hug his mom and dad the last time he saw them.

Alex stared, emotionless, at the faded, framed memory before placing it back on the table. And he turned out the light.

~ FIVE ~

FRANK STOOD WATCHING FROM the front door, as Alex walked out to the car, with 4-year-old Gracie and 6-year-old Tyler. Gracie turned back toward her dad, waving with a giggle in her voice.

"Bye, Daddy!"

"Don't wear Uncle Alex out too much!" Frank called out to Gracie with a chuckle, thoroughly enjoying his moment of busting his brother's chops.

Alex stopped behind the car, Tyler and Gracie in tow. "I was thinking ..." He opened the trunk, exposing a big, red snow sled.

Gracie and Tyler's eyes widened with surprise.

"You know - I can't take this with me ... I would look pretty silly on the beach, carrying this around, don't 'cha think?"

Tyler giggled. Gracie was pensive and raised an eyebrow at him.

He continued. "Your dad and I had some good times with this sled, a long time ago. It's yours now." Alex closed the trunk. He helped Gracie and Tyler climb into their seats and buckled them in.

Tyler asked, "Where are we going?"

"Where would you like to go?"

"How about *the North Pole*?" Gracie giggled again, from the back seat.

"Yeah! The North Pole!"

Alex had to do some quick thinking. "Hmm ... that might take too long; and then we might not be back by 4 O'clock ... when I told your mom and dad I'd have you home, and I don't think they would be very happy."

Tyler followed up with, "Can we take the sled to the park?"

Alex closed the car door. He started the Mustang and backed out of the driveway. Once out in the street, he shifted the car into drive and pointed forward.

"... *To the park*!

~ SIX ~

WALKING BACK TO the car, Alex noticed Gracie slowly beginning to lag behind as she observed her surroundings. She stopped on the path and stooped down, examining the snow-covered trail. Alex wandered over closer to where she had stopped. He studied her.

Gracie looked thoughtful for a moment, and then she motioned for him to come over. She was squatting over a patch of snow. Alex started to talk, but she interrupted him.

"Shhh ... I'm counting ...."

Alex inspected the snow and saw nothing. Bending over next to her, he struggled to see something. Still, he couldn't distinguish anything. "What are you counting, Gracie?"

She whispered as if she was keeping a secret. "Stars." She pointed to another patch of snow. "See?"

Alex was at a loss for words - unusual for him. He couldn't comprehend what she was talking about.

She picked up a stick and pointed to the first patch of snow. She looked back at Alex. "There. Stars."

He squinted his eyes, but all he could see was a mound of snow, with fresh bird tracks running through it. "The bird tracks?"

Gracie first frowned up at Alex, and then she grinned, as she corrected him. "Stars." She began counting again. "One, two, three, four, five, six, seven, eight, nine, ten ..." She hesitated, struggling to remember the rest of the numbers that followed.

She looked to Alex for help. And she whispered, "I have to count every star, so nobody gets left out."

Alex smiled. *I get it now. No bird track left behind.*

He prompted her to finish counting to twenty-three, but he still didn't understand how Gracie got *stars* from the tiny, scattered imprints in the snow.

Gracie looked back up at Alex with inquisitive eyes. "Don't you *love me to the moon and back* anymore?"

That little four-year-old just had a way of extracting a smile from him, like nobody else. Ordinarily Alex wasn't comfortable with outward shows of emotion and affection, but when it came to Gracie and Tyler, he never resisted.

"Why can't you stay here with us?"

He searched for words that could explain it all to a 4 year-old, but before he could open his mouth, Tyler surfaced from behind and bailed him out.

"Gracie's just going to miss you. Me too."

Alex stood and zipped up Tyler's jacket. "Me too."

While he buckled the kids in the car, his eyes instinctively glanced off toward the cliff to the houses. There appeared to be some activity in the vicinity of the old house.

The trio pulled out of the parking lot and Alex, out of curiosity, made the turn onto Edgecliff and around the corner toward the old place. He eased up on the gas slightly as they passed the circular drive, taking note that the door to the detached building next to the driveway was open.

He continued on to deliver the kids back home.

~ SEVEN ~

ALEX SLOWED TO 20 MPH as he approached the old house again. He noticed dozens of boxes, stacked high, out on the snow-covered driveway. He parked out at the curb, got out of his car and approached the garage. There he found Sarah, leaning over, struggling to carry a huge box.

"Having a Garage Sale?"

Sarah was startled. She looked up.

Alex tilted his dark tinted sunglasses, resting them on his head. He looked different in the afternoon sunlight.

His hazel eyes must have been set for stun as he trained them on Sarah. She froze, as the box she was carrying slipped from her grip, hitting the driveway. The sound of shattering glass filled the nippy air.

Alex cringed. "That can't be good."

Sarah looked disappointed. "That's the second one I've dropped." She pushed her glasses back up on the bridge of her nose and kneeled down beside the box. Her hair, pulled back in a ponytail, flipped over her head as she opened the flaps to see what had broken. She carefully pulled out a few large fragmented pieces of glassware and china.

"Crap; I don't know where to start."

"You know, this isn't exactly the most logical time to put this stuff out on the driveway." He picked up a box and showed her the bottom. "This old cardboard isn't going to hold out after it gets wet."

"You're right." She glanced up at him. "I should probably get this back in the garage, and worry more about the inside of the house." She crammed the paper and broken glass back into the box.

"I am meeting with a realtor this week. That doesn't give me much time. This can wait." Sarah picked up a large box and began walking toward the open garage.

Alex stopped her and reached over to take the box out of her arms. As his hand brushed hers, her heartbeat kicked up its pace and her thoughts about the garage vanished. She found herself leaning inward, toward him, hoping he might touch her hand again.

But when she caught herself, she quickly jerked her arm back. *What the hell did you do that for?*

Sarah wasn't what you would call an outwardly sexual woman, but she had a curious urge to touch him again. A thought she quickly dismissed, relinquishing the box to Alex.

He traveled in and out of the garage with more boxes and crates. With each trip, he began to notice more details inside. He placed the last carton against an old door at the back of the garage and pointed to it as he turned to leave. "And there's probably more stuff in this closet, too."

Sarah walked toward him and stopped at the door. She opened it, exposing a cold, dark stairwell. She explained, "This isn't a closet; it's the stairway to the attic, over the garage." She glanced up, her eyes widening. "I haven't been up there since I was a little girl."

Alex poked his head in. He quickly backed out and closed the door. "I don't see any kind of light coming in from up there."

Sarah hastily grabbed an old flashlight from the workbench and quickly disappeared inside the stairwell. The door slammed shut behind her. Alex reluctantly jumped back to the door.

"You can't just go up there by yourself!" Alex hollered through the closed door. He snorted in frustration as he realized Sarah was not coming back. "It's too dangerous; you don't know what you're going to find!"

She didn't answer him.

Jesus. Is she nuts? Alex impatiently flung open the old door to the attic. It creaked in protest. He stepped inside and he heard a loud slam behind him. It was dark and damp inside the stairwell and smelled of dust and old leaves. He could barely see a dim, orange glimmer from her flashlight. He waited a few seconds for his eyes to adjust. He was exasperated, but determined.

"Give me the flashlight." Again, Sarah did not answer him. A much more emphatic Alex followed with, "Give me the *Goddamn* flashlight!" A cobweb draped itself across his face, covering his open mouth. He frantically spit it out and brushed it away. He shuddered.

Sarah had already climbed the first three steep steps, when Alex pulled her back toward him, causing her to lose her balance. He caught her, breaking her fall, but she dropped the light.

And everything went dark.

A brief moment of awkward silence followed. They both felt the heat radiating off each other's bodies as Sarah struggled to become vertical again.

Alex fumbled in the dark, unintentionally sweeping his hand across Sarah's inner thigh, finally locating the flashlight on the step in front of her.

Sarah could feel her heart racing. She sucked in a little breath that got all tangled up in her chest.

Stay cool, Sarah. No need to broadcast to the world what you are thinking. It had been quite a dry spell since she had thought about having sex with anyone but every time she got close to Alex, it seemed to be on her mind.

He turned the flashlight back on and they could finally see where they were again.

Barely.

"You don't have any idea what you might find; there could be rodents living in this attic. You might even fall through something," Alex breathed, barely above a whisper.

Sarah offered up a look that told him she was going up there regardless of what he said. Alex inhaled deeply, then cautiously warned her,

"OK, but let me go first. Just in case."

Alex started up the narrow staircase, hearing the risers creak beneath his weight, with Sarah blindly holding his shirttail from behind.

What an ass. I should be at home, leafing through Florida beach brochures – not meeting my death in a dilapidated, old carriage house.

He aimed the fading light into every corner of the stairwell, straining his eyes, until he was sure it was safe to continue. They approached the top step, nearing the attic, the dwindling glow guiding the way.

The tiny stream of light arrived first; then Alex, followed by Sarah as they reached the top step. Alex pointed the flashlight across the floorboards, just as they found themselves in the attic. He aimed the feeble beam around the musty smelling room.

Sarah let out a gasp.

"What *is* this stuff?" Alex asked.

They cast their eyes upon dozens of large, old corrugated cardboard boxes, patterned with antiquity and dust, arranged in an organized fashion. Each box had a diagram attached to it.

Alex made his way through the steeply pitched attic, ducking so he wouldn't hit his head on one of the rough support beams.

When he moved closer, he noticed that some of the boxes were overflowing with large, colored glass balls, some attached to sockets - some lying loose. Several of the others were packed full of old electrical cords, some covered in cloth.

He started to count them, but the sheer number intimidated him. Standing against the last box was a tablet of yellowed paper with larger diagrams. Alex blew dust off the top page on the tablet. He looked over at Sarah.

"What was your grandfather; some kind of *spy*?"

Sarah rolled her eyes at Alex. She stepped across to a dirt-encrusted window on the other side of the sea of boxes and flung the shutters open, allowing a grimy glimmer of light to flow into the room.

She walked over to the carton closest to him. "Don't be ridiculous!" She reached in the box and pulled out a string of old, worn, outdoor Christmas lights, from the 1950's.

Her eyes lit up at the sight of it. She smiled as she recalled, "These are the lights my grandfather strung outside every Christmas, for as long as he lived here."

Alex held up another string. Raising an eyebrow, he probed, "These are the lights he used? You've got to be kidding!"

Sarah picked up a string, still in its original box. "My grandfather used the same lights, year after year. He always said it was a science." She straightened up and beamed at him, looking to Alex like she was a little girl. "Somehow, it always came together."

Alex looked in another box, picking up a smaller, flat one inside. "It doesn't look like these were ever opened."

Sarah peered over the box and answered. "Probably not; he always had extras, in case some of these went out. You know, back when these were new, if one light went out, the whole string went out." Alex laughed at the thought.

"Why didn't he just buy new lights, instead of using these old ones every year?"

Sarah leaned against the attic wall. "My grandfather first put up the display in 1954; the year they moved into this house." She let out a sigh. "He said that he didn't want to ever forget the look on my grandmother's face when she saw the lights for the first time that night." She fingered the outline of one of the diagrams and continued. "He looked forward to seeing the same look on her face every year."

For a moment, there was silence. Then her eyes lit up with her next words. "And that was all the incentive he needed to repeat history every Christmas."

Sarah put the light strings back and tucked in the tops of the boxes. She straightened up and appeared to be searching for something. "And somewhere, there are special bulbs. He mixed them in with the other lights; every year he used a different number of them, and changed where he put them on the strings."

She began unfolding the flaps on another box. "They were unique… the colored glass was so vibrant … and transparent … and they each blinked on and off, independently. I used to think they were stars."

Alex gave her a skeptical look.

She went on. "When he was all finished, it was my job to walk around with him and count every star, to make sure they were all *twinkling*." She opened another crumbling, flat carton, but set it aside.

Sarah continued rummaging through the pile of boxes. She grinned. "And then …"

Alex was curious. "Well, what is it?"

She held up a funny-looking series of hard plastic strips, attached to wedges of weathered hardwood, held together by wooden pegs and 10 strategically placed, single light bulbs, in the shape of a star.

She beamed at him. "It doesn't look like much now, but this is the original star that my grandfather always placed at the peak of the roof top."

Alex leaned in and strained his eyes, for a glimpse of the rickety old star.

"I remember, every year … we all held our breaths as we watched him make the climb to the rooftop. Nobody exhaled until he was safely back on the ground."

Alex took a little step backward. "Sounds dangerous to me. That top peak has a pretty steep slope."

Sarah examined the star closer. The power cord was frayed and barely attached at the base. She walked to a nearby electrical outlet on the wall.

Alex cautioned her. "I don't think that's a good idea."

Sarah ignored him, plugging the cord into the socket. It shorted out, sending fiery sparks into the air.

Alex quickly yanked the cord out of the outlet, catching his breath. "*Damn, Sarah!* He followed with a sigh of relief. "Are you *always* this impulsive?" He scolded her. "That could have caused a fire!"

She placed the star back in the box, adding it to the pile. "Sorry." She giggled at his reaction. "But it was the most magical time of the year. It just looked like Christmas."

Sarah joined Alex and began the descent back down to the ground level. She stepped out of the stairwell.

"After my grandfather died, the tradition sort-of died with him; even the neighbors began scaling down their own holiday decorations." She closed the door to the attic. "Maybe it was too big of a job, and everybody just got tired."

"Then the neighbors began moving away." Sarah walked out to the Mustang with Alex. She smiled at him as he opened his car door. "Thanks for stopping by … and for putting it all into perspective for me. The house comes first; then the garage."

But before he could take his seat, Sarah's facial expression changed to a puzzled look. She searched the pockets of her coat for something.

"What's wrong?" Alex asked her.

She looked back at him. "I must have dropped my phone. Never mind; it'll turn up. I'll look for it later." But after a moment, she reconsidered and asked him, "Can I call my phone from yours? I honestly have no idea where I could have left it."

Alex reached in his pocket and handed her his phone. Sarah noted his business card, attached to the leather case.

Alex Wagner -Senior Communications Specialist
Oz Communications

Sarah keyed in her number and they waited, straining their ears, until they finally caught wind of a ring tone.

She raced back into the garage, following the music. In her haste, she neglected to give the phone back to Alex. Sarah discovered the weathered receiver on top of a large tarp, in a back corner of the garage, and held it up triumphantly for Alex to see.

He stepped back into the garage to retrieve his phone.

Alex squeezed past the mountain of boxes, brushing against the loosely draped tarp. It moved a little, exposing a corner of a large metal object.

He jumped, and then he cautiously peeled back the sheet a little more. He blinked his eyes in disbelief. Alex couldn't move.

Sarah reached around him and hastily dropped the remainder of the tarp on the floor of the garage, revealing a 1955 Chevy Bel Aire.

"My grandfather's car. He bought it right after they moved into this house." She ran her hand along the right fender. "This was … *his baby.* My grandmother joked that if he'd ever had to choose between her and this car, he'd pick the car."

She laughed at the thought. "But, we all knew that wasn't true."

Alex slowly walked around the car, amazed that, despite the layers of filth covering everything else in the garage, the exterior was shiny, as if it had just been waxed. He moved on, peering through the windows.

Sarah followed Alex. "He did have a way with cars … a *sixth sense.*"

The interior of the Bel Aire looked new. Alex stopped at the driver's door. "When was the last time it was driven?"

"I don't think it has left the garage since he died; I guess twenty years or so." She let out a little giggle. "When he was alive, he was so nervous when anybody else touched it, everybody was afraid to drive it."

"Ironically, he said he looked forward to teaching me to drive in it when I was old enough." Sarah traced the edge of the windshield with her index finger. "Timing is everything, isn't it? Obviously, *that* didn't work out, although I spent many Sunday afternoons, helping him wax it."

Alex adjusted the drivers' side mirror, amazed that it, too, didn't need to be dusted off.

"And my grandmother just never moved it after he died."

Alex looked over at her with concern. "Sarah, a classic like this ... needs to be started once in a while, or the engine will seize. Oil can settle in the crank case." He opened the door and leaned in and he muttered aloud to himself, "The battery's dead - for sure."

Alex pivoted and placed himself in the driver's seat. Positioned a little too far back for his legs, Alex adjusted the seat closer and placed his hands on the steering wheel, as if he was about to start the engine. He turned and looked back to the driveway, then to Sarah.

"Move off to the side. I'm going to try to get her out in the fresh air, if that's okay with you."

She stepped onto the walkway and watched as Alex put the car in neutral, pushed off the garage floor with his foot, and then let the Bel Aire roll out onto the driveway.

He turned his head and shot her a grin.

Sarah reached in her jacket pocket, and handed a keychain to Alex. "One of these might be the right one. See what you think."

He looked at a few keys before finding one that he thought might work. He placed the key in the ignition.

It was a perfect fit. He held his breath and turned the key. "I hope this doesn't do any more damage."

But to his surprise, the engine fired up without any hesitation at all. Alex's mouth dropped open in disbelief. *"You've got to be kidding!"*

The engine purred. Alex smiled. He sat back and relaxed in the seat for a moment, before driving the Bel Aire, slowly, back into the garage. His heart raced as he turned off the ignition. He stepped out slowly and handed the keys back to Sarah.

Alex stared back at the car. "I just don't believe it. The tires aren't even flat!" He eyed her with suspicion. "Are you *sure* it hasn't been driven?" Alex covered up the car again with the tarp and patted the hood gently.

Sarah nodded as she reached for her phone.

He rubbed his chin and swept Sarah's phone from her hand. He turned it over. "You really should get a new one. This is pretty pathetic, you know," he said, studying Sarah's scratched up, worn, outdated phone. Alex handed the phone to Sarah and walked toward the front of the garage.

Sarah shrugged and tagged along behind him. "I don't think it's all that necessary to have every latest and greatest gadget. As long as it works; who cares?"

Alex looked at Sarah. "Does it?"

"Does it *what*?"

"Work. Does it *work*?"

She answered him, sheepishly. "Well, *most* of the time. I always get incoming calls and I can call out. Sometimes the display breaks up ... and it doesn't always show me missed calls."

She warmed her hands in her pockets and gave him a grin. "But other than that, it's *perfectly fine*."

He rolled his eyes at her. "I rest my case."

Alex pointed at the car as he backed out of the garage. "Just make sure you sell that to somebody who will appreciate what they're getting."

Sarah smiled halfheartedly. "I've been wondering how I'm going to bring up the subject with my grandmother again. She doesn't want to sell it, but I don't really have a choice." She looked up at him. "What do you think it's worth?"

Alex hesitated at the door and walked back to the old Chevy. "I'm not sure. I'd have to do some research. One of the guys I work with restores vintage cars. I'll see what he says. Would you mind if I took a couple of pictures?"

"Take as many as you want."

Alex pulled out his phone and began snapping images of the interior and exterior of the car as Sarah continued talking.

"I am going to stop in to see Irene tomorrow." She frowned slightly. "If I'm lucky, she will recognize me. One of the reasons I had to move her to the facility ..." Sarah went on with sadness in her voice. "... She started hallucinating - imagining and hearing things that just weren't there."

Alex snapped the last of the pictures and stopped to look over at her.

"At times she acts like I'm not even there. But other times she's so bright." Sarah sighed. "She's been so strong her whole life ... but now, sometimes I think she's giving up."

Alex gave her an empathetic smile.

She turned to him and asked, "Would you consider meeting me there and helping me explain that it's worth something and she should consider selling it? She might listen if she thinks you know something about cars."

Alex brushed his hair out of his eyes, giving himself time to come up with a suitable reply. He was a little uncomfortable, but he agreed.

"Umm ... sure - I can try."

Sarah pulled out a scrap of paper from her jeans pocket and scribbled on it. She handed it to him. "Here's the address of where she is. Don't worry if you can't make it - no pressure. I will be there around 5:30."

Alex glanced down at the address and nodded. He put the paper in his pocket, jumped into the Mustang and turned the ignition. "Be careful up in that attic."

"I doubt I'll even go back up there." She laughed. "Thanks again."

Alex backed out of the driveway.

~ EIGHT ~

SARAH OPENED HER EYES, revealing the warm sunlight streaming in through the Dotted Swiss sheers. She stretched and yawned, taking in the lazy morning. But the peaceful tranquility of daybreak was soon shattered by a combination of pounding at the front door, and the incessant chiming of the bell.

Sarah jumped out of bed, staring at the clock.

Really? ... It's only 7 am! Who has something that important that it can't wait a few hours?

She grabbed a robe and covered her shorts and t-shirt as she flew down the main stairs. She reached the front door and peeked through the side window curtain.

Sarah recognized Mary, from the real estate firm she was working with. Sleepily annoyed, she opened the door. "Mary? Uh - how are you?" Mary was more than eager to get started.

"No time for idle chit-chat. We have a lot to do this morning, if I am going to get this place sold!" She juggled a red clipboard with her matching travel coffee mug.

"I've done some of the work from outside already but I need to see what I'm up against, inside this dinosaur," she said, slurping her hazelnut-infused java.

Mary didn't wait to be invited inside; she pushed her way into the living room. Sarah joined the woman, who was already examining the floor-to-ceiling stone fireplace. "Paint!"

Sarah's eyes followed the stone from the floor to the ceiling. Confused, she looked to Mary for clarification. "*Paint?*"

Mary quickly shifted gears and moved on, barely taking the time to answer Sarah's question. "*This is just crying out for paint*. Buyers *love* everything if it's painted a crisp white!"

Sarah's jaw dropped. "But it's stone ..."

Mary didn't comment or stop. She moved on to the woodwork surrounding the picture window with the view of downtown Cleveland. She examined the window sashes, scrutinizing every detail, without even noticing the spectacular scene.

Sarah joined Mary at the window. She stopped and sat on the upholstered seat cushion. She hugged her knees to her chest and gazed out over the lake. Sarah sighed. "This is the best seat in the whole city."

Mary abruptly snapped the curtains closed, trapping Sarah in between the heavy fabric and the window. Sarah disappeared behind the drapes.

"Hey! I'm still in here!"

Mary rushed off toward the kitchen. "Those will have to go!"

Sarah flung the curtains back open and jumped out, following Mary. "Maybe they are a little outdated ... but, the view?"

Mary ignored Sarah's comment and continued through the house.

The sound of a horrified, exasperated Mary echoed from the kitchen. "*Oh, No!* This will *all* have to go!"

Sarah frowned and rolled her eyes as she reluctantly joined her.

Mary shrieked. "How *old* are these appliances? Oh, honey; this is an *absolute real estate nightmare!*"

The sound of Mary's voice faded into background noise as Sarah did her best to pretend she was listening.

~ NINE ~

ALEX'S CAR DOOR OPENED and he stepped out into the parking lot with a simple bouquet of flowers, wrapped in green waxed paper. Sarah approached him with a quizzical smile.

"Does your grandmother like flowers?"

She smiled. "Irene *adores* flowers!"

He held the bouquet out to her, but she shook her head. "It will mean more to her if you give them to her yourself." Sarah explained further, with pure enthusiasm, as she continued toward the entrance. "My Grandfather used to bring her flowers every Friday. She's going to love them!"

Alex followed her into the building and past the nurses' station. He paused just outside, while Sarah knocked on the doorframe. He studied Sarah's eyes; they held such hope. She motioned for Alex to follow her. They entered the room and Alex turned his attention to the woman in the bed by the window.

Irene was reclining slightly in her bed, asleep. She looked very angelic, considerably younger than a woman in her 80's. Alex was surprised by how naturally beautiful she was.

Irene soon sensed there were people in the room and opened her eyes. She smiled when she saw Sarah walking toward her. Holding out her hand to Sarah, she smiled an even bigger smile.

Sarah gazed into Irene's baby blue eyes and said, "Grandmother - I have someone I'd like you to meet."

Irene's eyes shifted and found Alex. He was holding the flowers, looking a little lost. Her face brightened. Her eyes lit up at the sight of such a handsome young man, bringing her flowers.

"This is Alex."

"Alex." Irene nodded her head. "What a *nice* name." She looked intently over at the flowers in his hand. "Are those for me?"

Alex gently held out the flowers to Irene.

She looked over at Sarah and glowed. "Is it Friday already?" she asked with a sweet smile, placing the flowers closer to her nose, savoring their fragrance. "Thank you, Alex."

Sarah's expression became slightly serious with her next sentence. "I asked Alex to find out what Grandfather's car is worth."

Irene stiffened a little at the thought. A nurse appeared at the doorway and stopped. She apologized. "Sorry to interrupt. Sarah, can I have you sign some new paperwork out at the desk?"

Sarah put her purse on the table and told Irene, "I'll be right back." She walked into the hallway.

When Alex started to follow her, Irene called him back. "Alex, won't you come and sit by me?"

He walked back into the room and sat at Irene's bedside. Her face held no expression.

"Paperwork." She exhaled. "I guess my life has been reduced to a *mere* pile of papers." She made direct eye contact with Alex.

He was drawn in. Was it her beauty or her genuine sincerity? Or both? He wasn't sure what spell he was under.

Irene seemed to discover a renewed strength. She sat up a little more and repositioned herself. She gradually became very focused and bright. And happy. Alex saw Sarah in her face.

"So, what makes you so sure that old car is worth selling?"

Alex opened the folder he had brought in and held out a picture of the car from a magazine for her to see. He leaned in closer to her. He found it difficult to contain his excitement. "That car is in fantastic condition! I have a friend who restores classic cars. I showed him a picture. He said he's never seen one in that good of shape."

He paused, and then he rolled his eyes, continuing the thought. "And when I told him it started with no hesitation after all these years, I thought he was going to have a heart attack."

Irene became quiet. She handed the picture back to Alex. Their eyes met again. She leaned in toward Alex and spoke in a soft, yet firm tone.

"They think I'm just a crazy old lady, but …" She took Alex's hand and squeezed it. "I never should have told anybody … but Alex … I *know* I heard the car running late at night." She closed her eyes and opened them again. "And *not just once.*"

Irene gently released Alex's hand. She looked down at her wrinkled hand and spoke just above a whisper. "I may be old, but I can still tell the difference between what's real and what isn't."

Alex couldn't help feeling compassion for what she must have been going through.

But Irene quickly recovered and changed the subject. She patted Alex's hand, giving him a smile. "So, Alex ... What's your story?"

"My *story*?" He raised an eyebrow.

Irene laughed as she took both of Alex's hands in hers. "Everybody has a story. It starts with your family," she told him with a wink.

Alex stood and took a few steps to the side. Nervously placing his hands in his pockets, he began. "I'm from Cleveland."

"And your parents?"

He turned and faced the window. "My mother and father died in a highway accident when I was 12."

Irene's face dropped. Her eyes filled with empathy. "Oh, Alex, I am so sorry."

Alex sat back down in the chair next to Irene. He stared, showing no emotion. "I thought my life was over." He closed his eyes. "My brother - Frank ... he was 20 years old ... gave up his own life and raised me. He took me in and became my parents ..." Alex became silent again.

Irene studied his body language. "Well then … he must be a *very special* young man. *Just look at you!*"

Irene noticed Alex appeared to be deepening in thought. She engaged him further. "What do you do, Alex?"

He looked at her again. "Well, in a couple of weeks, I'll be on my way to Florida."

"Florida?"

"That's where the money is. I am opening my own communications business. I can't wait to move and get started."

"Why the big hurry?"

"My plan is to be the most successful entrepreneur in my field, before I am 35," he explained.

Drawing Alex into her soul through her eyes, Irene said, "Oh honey - be careful what you wish for." The light in her eyes intensified. "You can be in such a hurry to get to your future that you miss the present."

Sarah appeared in the doorway. She walked into the room, sat at Irene's side, and squeezed her hand. The bond they shared was unmistakable.

Irene shifted gears and smiled back at Sarah.

~ TEN ~

SARAH GOT OUT OF her car, weighed down with bags from her shopping trip, gabbing on her phone.

"Well, I think I found some curtains that will work. I mean, I don't have to like them *personally*. It's not like it's *my* house." She stepped onto the landing and juggled the bags from one side to the other.

After a pause, while the person on the other end of the line spoke to her, she continued. "Yes, I should be back at work in a couple of weeks."

Sarah put the phone in the pocket of her jacket and pulled out the keys to the house. She unlocked and entered the house through the front door, balancing on one leg while she closed the door with the other foot.

The bags tumbled from her arms onto the floor in the foyer as she walked through. She tossed the keys into the dish on the table, and backtracked to pick up the bags from the floor.

Sarah heard a knock at the front door. She opened it and stepped outside. There was nobody there. She moved down a step, to get a better look. Still nothing.

The wind off the lake gusted and whipped through her hair. She turned, frantically trying to dash back in time, but she was not fast enough. She reached it just in time to watch the door slam shut. She tried to open it, but it was just as she suspected.

Locked.

Sarah walked around the outside of the house. She inspected all the windows. She desperately tried the other two doors. Eventually, she found herself back at the front door. She shivered.

Dumbass! How could you be so stupid?

Luckily, she reached in her jacket pocket and found her phone. She began reading through the contacts, but there wasn't one name in the list that could have been helpful. They were all out of town.

"Jess ... Brad ... oh, this will *never work*! You are all 500 miles away!" she said aloud, to herself, in frustration. She started to return the phone to her pocket, when she remembered something.

"Wait! Maybe Alex's number is in the missed calls."

Sarah searched back through the phone again, recalling that she had asked Alex to call her phone on Sunday. She spotted an unfamiliar number from Sunday afternoon. She hit the send button while she paced back and forth in front of the house, waiting.

"I hope this is your number, Alex." She shook the snow out of her hair.

~ ~ ~ ~ ~

Alex was on the couch, flipping through a magazine with a tropical beach on the cover. He saw that he had a call, but it wasn't a number he recognized. At first, he didn't answer it, but he reconsidered and caught it just before it went to his voicemail.

"Hello?"

"Alex?"

He recognized Sarah's voice. "*Sarah - is that you?* Hey ... what's up?"

She immediately apologized. "I am so sorry to bother you like this. I found your number in my missed calls." She shivered through the phone.

"I don't know anybody here. I heard this knock at the door, and when I went outside, the door locked behind me. I didn't know who else to call." There was a pause. "Could you help me get back into the house? The keys are in there and ..."

Alex interrupted her. "I'm about 10 minutes from you. I'll be right there. Can you go to a neighbor's house and wait for me inside?"

Sarah was emphatic. "*No!* I don't want them to know I locked myself out." She sighed and finished with, "What kind of a first impression would that make?"

That made absolutely no sense to Alex at all. He shook his head. *Okay; if she wants to freeze to death, that's her prerogative.*

"Alright, I'll be there as soon as I can. Try to stay warm." He ended the call, grabbed his jacket off the back of the chair and opened the front door.

~ ELEVEN ~

THE MUSTANG WAS IN the driveway for only ten seconds before the headlights went dark. The door opened. Alex stepped out onto the pavement and met Sarah, who was already half way down the drive. She smiled and shrugged.

A sudden, puffball of air from behind caught Sarah off-guard, throwing her balance off, pushing her into Alex. He grabbed hold of her arm just before she slipped on the ice.

"Whoa – be careful." He laughed, as Sarah regained her footing and they continued to the front of the old house.

As they stepped onto the landing, another, much stronger, lake breeze picked up, blowing debris against the foundation of the house. A stray gust caught a large branch that had fallen from a nearby tree, and flung it hard, against the front door.

Alex bent down to pick up the branch. He examined it and handed it to Sarah, with a know-it-all grin. "Here's your mysterious, *knock on the door.*"

After a fruitless attempt to find a way to get in through the front of the house, he stepped around to the side with Sarah close behind. He rattled the kitchen door and examined the window; they were tighter than a drum.

A two-part window, up high on the back of the house, seemed to be his last resort, short of breaking out an entire window. He jumped up a few times, to see if it had possibilities. The third time, he noticed there was already a small crack in the left corner of the bottom pane. He turned to Sarah and asked,

"Is there a ladder out in the garage?"

She led Alex to the unlocked garage and she answered. "I'm sure there is." Sarah opened the garage and chuckled. "Everything else is in there." Sure enough, there was a ladder, right out in the open.

Alex leaned the ladder against the house and stepped up, one rung at a time, finally reaching the window. He used his pocketknife, and cut the screen off the entire frame while Sarah watched impatiently from the ground.

He broke out the little cracked section of pane and managed to reach his gloved hand in at an angle to be able to turn the lock on the window. The sash popped loose.

With one leg through the opening, he looked back at Sarah. "I'll go in and let you in through the front."

Once inside, Alex jumped down from the sink and located a light switch. He searched around the kitchen for a doorway leading to the front of the house.

He walked through the old house, turning lights on, noticing the fine detail and character of the place. He ran his hand along the beautifully carved woodwork and over the cool, stone fireplace as he passed them in the dining room.

Alex found himself in a huge living room, where he saw another fireplace. The room looked like it hadn't been touched in at least 20 years.

Sarah gave him a victorious smile as he opened the front door to let her inside. He quickly pointed to a tray on a table by the door holding the set of keys he remembered from Sunday afternoon and astutely advised her,

"You'd better take these now, so you don't lock yourself out again."

Sarah looked over to where Alex was pointing. She shook her head and she replied. "Oh, those are my grandfather's keys. They have always been there."

Alex stared back at her, puzzled.

Sarah continued. "My grandmother insisted on keeping them right there, in that tray, on that table, all these years ... even after he died."

"Why did she do that?"

"I'm not really sure. Maybe she felt that, as long as his keys were still here, on the table, he could come home." She walked over to another table, by the opposite side of the door and pointed. "I put *my* keys on *this* table."

Alex noticed that her set was smaller; it was very similar to the first set, but with a few keys missing. He continued to look around, studying the old place.

Sarah disappeared into the kitchen. She called out, "I'm making coffee. Want some?"

He joined her. He watched her as she pulled out an old-fashioned percolator from a little pantry closet. Alex chuckled; his mother had used one just like it … ancient.

"Thanks; I'll have a little." Alex looked around and walked toward the back door. "I'll board this window up for you, until you can have it repaired. I saw something in the garage that will work."

He vanished, and then reappeared with a piece of plywood, nails and a hammer. As Alex finished the repair, he commented, "Things just aren't made like this anymore. Solid. Somebody took a lot of pride in his work with this house." He climbed back down from the counter and left the hammer on the table.

Sarah opened the overhead cupboard and pulled out two cups. She handed Alex one and poured coffee for them both. She pointed to the carton of milk and sugar, sitting on the kitchen table. He took a little of each and stirred them into his coffee.

Alex followed Sarah to the living room. She settled in a chair by the big picture window framing the Cleveland skyline. He wandered over to the window and stared out at the view a moment before sitting in the chair opposite her.

"I can sure see why they bought this house."

Sarah stood again and perched herself in the window seat. She curled up and leaned against the frame. "My grandparents loved this place. I thought they'd live here forever."

Alex rolled his eyes and shook his head at the *forever* comment.

She went on. "They had some road blocks along the way…" She looked wistful before finishing. "… but they were *meant* to be."

Sarah turned to Alex and she added, "They met, in Dayton, right before he shipped out during the war. Oh, I already told you that, didn't I?" She took another sip from her cup.

"They wrote letters for three months; they're still in the attic, I think." She sat up straight and leaned in toward Alex. "Then, when my grandmother moved to Cleveland, they lost touch somehow. She said she stopped getting his forwarded letters." Sarah slowly moved the cup back and forth between her hands. "She was heartbroken."

Intrigued, Alex surprised himself by his interest in the story. He listened intently as Sarah continued.

"Eventually, she started dating again. She was even engaged to be married." Sarah held her cup in both hands and rested against the window. "The night before her wedding, Winston ..." she paused. That's grandpa's name, arrived back home to Dayton, with a shattered ankle. He asked around and learned that Irene had moved to Cleveland." She took another sip.

Alex paused, the coffee cup inches from his mouth. "Did he know she was getting married?"

Sarah swallowed her coffee quickly and she shook her head, with a smile. "Not yet." She set her cup on the table and then leaned back against the window, silhouetted by the city lights. "He didn't even unpack. He sent a wire to her parents and set out on a one-man mission.

She finished off her coffee. "Winston jumped in his car and made the grueling drive to Cleveland."

Alex winced at the thought of the pain; his own ankle ached with empathy.

Sarah's eyes widened. "And there he found her, in the middle of an argument, on the front porch with her fiancé, Todd, one of his buddies from school – they had even enlisted together!"

She giggled. "I guess there was quite a scene. Todd was supposed to have been passing some information along to Irene for Winston; which he, of course, never did."

Alex sat up in the chair. "So, what happened?"

"Winston didn't kill Todd, although I think he wanted to. He just broke his nose." She sighed. "By the time everybody's stories came out, all my grandparents cared about was that grandpa was okay, and that they were together again." Sarah pushed her hair behind her ears and went on. "They were married a month later. And the rest is history."

She smiled and stood. "It almost sounds like a movie, doesn't it?"

Sarah continued. "They scrimped and saved; living in a tiny apartment for 9 years. Then, one day, my grandfather was on his morning walk along the lakeshore, and saw the *For Sale* sign in the front yard. He talked the man into taking the sign down until he had the chance to show it to my grandmother."

Alex waited for the rest of the story.

"The sign never went back up."

Sarah's phone rang from in the kitchen. She ran to answer it. Alex continued to drink his coffee, peering out at the framed Cleveland panorama. He couldn't help studying the scene.

"Yes, I can. Where is it?" She returned to the living room, feverishly writing on the back of an envelope. Then she tucked it into her purse. "Ok - I will be there."

She ended the call and gave Alex a perplexed look. "Mary wants me to meet her for dinner on Friday. She's got an appraisal and some suggestions to help get this house sold."

"Your realtor?" Alex asked.

She nodded. "I'd like to have this all over with and sold by the end of the year."

Alex put his cup on the table and looked around the huge living room. "That's not a lot of time. But then, I don't see a lot that you need to do - except clearing the personal stuff out." He touched a floor-to-ceiling column and lifted his eyes toward the vaulted ceiling. "And a little TLC."

Sarah returned to the picture window and faced the lake. She gazed out at the water, with its dancing lattice of lights, and shook her head. "I have a little over three weeks left of vacation time I'm using. I can't do this long-distance - I owe my grandparents that much."

Her phone rang again.

Alex glanced down at it. He read the name on the screen - *Brad*. He picked up her phone, walked it over to the window, and handed it to her.

She looked at the caller ID, and placed the phone on the ledge. She ignored it and continued looking out the window, offering no explanation. Alex wondered why, but didn't say anything. He sat back down in the chair.

Sarah looked up at the unevenly hanging curtains above the window. Leaning into the well, she studied the curtain rod from the inside. "That's not right. It's bent. If I don't fix this now, the new ones will never fit." Sarah stepped up onto the window seat and jumped up, trying to reach the rod."

"Do you need help?"

She grasped the curtain rod and yanked it off the brackets. She shook her head and glanced back at Alex. Still standing on the seat, Sarah began unthreading the fabric from the rod. She was curious about Alex and who he was. "So ... you're a communications genius?"

"No; I'm *not a genius*," Alex smirked. "I design communication and network contingency plans for companies, in the event something should go wrong."

Sarah wrinkled her nose. "Sounds complicated; not like me; you can't get any more uncomplicated than me. As long as my computer turns on, I'm happy."

Alex took another sip of coffee, and raised an eyebrow at Sarah.

"You don't think what *you* do is complicated?"

She pulled on the length of the bent metal pole. "Sure, if you think just opening my mouth and talking is complicated. Doing voice-overs and cartoon voices just pays the bills. It's not what I really want to do," Sarah said with a smile, looking off in the distance.

"What do you want to do?"

Sarah looked a little hesitant, studied his face, and then she went for it. "I want to create; I really want to design costumes." She began pushing the curtain rod back through the fabric rod pocket.

Alex responded with a blank expression.

She sensed Alex wasn't relating to what she had just told him. She frowned. "Well; *somebody* has to be the wardrobe designer in the theatre. And movies, too." She got quiet. "I *knew* you'd think it was dumb."

"I never said it was dumb - I just never thought about who does that stuff." He smiled at her. "So, why aren't you ... *designing*?"

Sarah tensed and rolled her eyes in frustration. "Do you know how many wardrobe designers there are in New York City?" She glared at the ceiling. "*Hundreds!* They're all 21 years old, and they're all looking for the same job I am, and will do *anything* to get it."

Alex placed his cup on the table again and he probed. "So ... doing cartoon voices and voice-overs can't be *that* bad, can it?"

Sarah stretched higher to reach the bracket. Alex's voice faded. She bristled, momentarily forgetting where she was, and she took herself back two months in time.

60

Sarah is sitting at a table for two. She is dressed for a special occasion. She is wearing glasses, nervously waiting for someone to join her.

In walks Brad, a very striking man - the kind of man who draws attention everywhere he goes. When Brad walks into a room, everybody notices.

He knows it and loves it.

He looks around the room for admiring glances as he approaches the table, flashing a phony smile.

Sarah suddenly realizes that she is wearing her glasses, and quickly snatches them from her face, hiding them under the folded linen napkin, on the table. She pats the napkin and fluffs it, in an attempt to cover what's underneath.

Brad seats himself at the table. Sarah looks at him, for some kind of sign. He takes her hand, as if to be offering condolences.

Sarah recognizes the familiar look, quickly pulling back her hand, disappointedly.

"No?"

Brad replies in a condescending tone, with a fake, toothy grin. "This just isn't the right production for you, Sarah."

Looking down, emotionless, Sarah asks him, "Brad; will there ever be a right production for me?"

Insincerely, he pats Sarah's hand. "Sweetheart; these things take time."

Sarah is visibly upset.

Brad glances around the room to see if they are being observed. In a disapproving voice, he tells her, "You need to be patient."

Sarah picks up the napkin and throws it in her lap, exposing her glasses, on the table.

"Haven't you gotten rid of those yet?" He asks, eyeing her suspiciously.

Sarah fidgets, dropping the glasses into her purse, under the table and tells him, "I haven't had the time."

The waitress brings a bottle of champagne with two glasses and places them on the table; she pours the bubbly into each of the glasses, smiles at them and leaves. Sarah raises her glass, as if she is waiting for a toast.

Brad hastily takes a sip after they clink glasses. "Sweetheart; I hate to leave so soon, but I've got a last-minute appointment."

Sarah is seething. "Now? I thought we were going to spend my birthday together! That's why we met here!"

Without hesitation, Brad gets up from the table, and gives Sarah a quick kiss on the top of the head. "I'll make it up to you, soon. Happy Birthday."

He hands her a small box. She looks up at him; he is still standing at the table. "Do you want me to open it? Now?"

Brad appears somewhat disinterested and in a hurry, but he sits back down.

Sarah looks at Brad and gives him a weak smile. "It's OK; go to your appointment. I'll be fine."

Brad jumps up eagerly, patting her hand. "Happy Birthday, Sweetheart."

Sarah reaches to touch his arm with her other hand, but he has already slipped away, giving her his signature "wave" as he exits the dining room.

Sarah is left at the table, all alone. She slowly opens the elaborately wrapped package, revealing a little purple velvet box. She opens it and finds a pair of expensive diamond earrings. Sarah smiles a little smile, closing the box, whispering, "I don't have pierced ears."

She blankly takes a sip of her champagne.

The waitress approaches the table and exclaims, "I saw them! What beautiful earrings! Would you like a menu; or another glass?"

Sarah quickly guzzles the remainder her champagne and looks up at the waitress. "Oh, I think I've had enough." Sarah stands, leaving more than enough money to cover their drinks and a tip, on the table. She dons her coat and walks out of the restaurant.

Moments later, outside on the street in the rain, Sarah flags down a cab. She runs, covering her head with her purse. As she reaches to open the door, a reflection in the window stops her. She sees another taxi, stopped across the street, about 500 feet from the corner.

It's Brad. She turns to get a better look. He is opening the door for a young woman, obviously dressed for a night on the town. He climbs in the taxi after her, and it pulls away.

Sarah ducks back out of the cab, telling the driver, "Wait here for just a minute; I forgot something."

The cab sits, idling, while Sarah quickly walks back into the restaurant. She passes the hostess counter and approaches the waitress at her station.

"I'm sorry; forgive me. I don't think I left you a big enough tip." She reaches in her purse, taking out the purple box. She places it firmly in her hand. "Here." Sarah exits the restaurant, leaving the waitress standing there, with her mouth hanging open, in disbelief.

Without realizing it, Sarah had trapped herself somewhere in between her pent-up anger at the past and the present moment. She dropped the curtains, and instinctively launched herself at someone who wasn't there.

Fortunately, Alex sensed her distress and he was close enough to her, so he was able to jump up onto the window seat and grab her before she fell. She resisted, fighting him, her hands curled into fists, so he wrapped his arms tightly around her and held her still.

Sarah returned to the present. Realizing she was locked tightly in Alex's embrace, she remembered what she had just done. She looked around the room.

"What are you doing?" he asked her.

"I'm not sure." She was embarrassed.

"You sure have a funny way of thanking me for helping you tonight." Alex loosened his hold and then he studied her. He smiled - a smile that came so suddenly Sarah actually felt the wind knocked out of her.

Alex jumped down from the ledge and held out his hand to her. Still a little unsteady on her feet, she was hesitant to jump. He reached up and placed his hands on her waist. With no effort, he lifted her back down to the floor.

He looked at her. "Were you trying to hurt me?" He smiled at her silent humiliation. He added, "Because if you were, you failed."

Sarah was grateful to Alex but she found herself suddenly defensive. She barked, "I may not fit everybody else's idea of what I should look and be like, but there's got to be something out there for me!"

Alex was taken aback. He looked at her, in surprise.

Suddenly realizing that she had just gone off on an innocent stranger, she apologized immediately. She blushed. "*Wow*. I am so sorry. I didn't mean to get so angry." She shifted her eyes downward, then back to Alex. "There are people ... who love to take every opportunity to remind me that I have flaws."

She tried to explain further, but Alex interrupted her. "I didn't mean to upset you."

Sarah walked past the window and picked up her cup, heading for the kitchen. She ran water in the cup and then placed it in the sink

Alex followed her and added his to the pile. "Thanks for the coffee."

Sarah smiled. "And thank you for getting me into the house. I don't know what I would have done without you." She followed Alex to the door, wondering what he must have been thinking of her, after that little episode.

He faced her. "If you need anything else, give me a call." He paused and added, "I'll be around for a couple of weeks, anyway."

"Are you going away for the holidays?"

Alex became animated with his response to her question. "I'm leaving for Miami on the 22nd, to finalize where I'm going to live; then I will be out of here for good, by January."

Sarah gave him a perplexed look. He realized he hadn't told her about his plans.

"I am moving ... opening my own consulting business, in Florida. I have wanted this for over 7 years. It's finally going to happen."

"But *Florida*?"

"I can't wait to live somewhere where the weather is predictable -and warm most of the time. It makes me so happy to know that I have stepped into my last snowdrift."

Sarah giggled at him. "Well, then I'm happy for you."

They exchanged a brief, friendly hug; he stepped out and disappeared down the driveway. Sarah shook her head and laughed.

Then she closed the door.

~ TWELVE ~

CLAIRE STRUTTED INTO the downtown café. Extraordinarily unblemished, presenting herself in an unbuttoned winter coat, over a tight fitting skirt and low-cut cashmere sweater, she stopped traffic.

Everybody noticed Claire and she knew it. Bursting with self-confidence, she slid in between Mike and Alex and positioned herself on the empty stool. She smiled at Alex.

Struggling not to look down at her ample cleavage as he assisted her with her coat, Alex had a hard time focusing while speaking.

"What will I have?" He turned beet-red. In a flustered voice, he attempted to correct his Freudian slip.

"I mean, what will *you* have?"

Outside on the street, Mary and Sarah sidestepped couples lingering in front of the café window. They ambled through the bar, on their way to the dining room.

Sarah noticed Alex at the bar with his friends, but she did not want to intrude. She couldn't help observing Claire - how she leaned back provocatively on the bar. And how she seemed to be all over Alex.

She has to be his girlfriend. She frowned and looked away. *Well, I guess there's no accounting for taste.*

Mary motioned to the dining room. "You're going to love the food here. It's a little like New York, LA and Europe - all rolled into one."

The hostess seated them at a table, next to the pillars separating the bar area from the dining room. Sarah quietly observed the bar activity from her table as Mary unfolded her paperwork.

"So, here's what I think we need to do."

Sarah probed, reviewing the papers. "Mary - is all of this really necessary?" She flipped through the last few pages. "Isn't there a chance that somebody might just like the house for what it is?" She rested her hand on the stack.

"This is going to cost a lot of money."

The waitress delivered a basket of chips to the table scribbled their drink order on the pad.

Sarah and Mary's conversation was interrupted by an apparent disturbance from the bar. Claire had bumped her glass and her drink had spilled on her sweater.

Claire shrieked and jumped up from the table. "This is a *three hundred* dollar sweater!"

Alex tried to help. "It's just a little spill. We can have it cleaned."

Mike quickly stood and tried to blot it with napkins. "Claire - it's not *that* bad." She pushed his hand away from her chest and rushed off to the ladies room, visibly upset.

Back on the opposite side of the cafe, Sarah excused herself from the table. "Mary, I will be right back. I need to visit the ladies room." Sarah hurried off.

When she opened the door, Claire was at the sink, frantically trying to scrub the stain out of her sweater. From a distance, Sarah noticed her own reflection, next to Claire's, in the mirror. She couldn't help feeling out of place, next to Claire's sophisticated beauty and expensive clothing.

Sarah reached in her purse and took out a packet. She tore it open, removed a wet towlette and held it out to Claire. "Here. I think this will get that stain out of your sweater."

Claire seized the wipe from Sarah and scowled, "Thanks. I cannot believe those guys spilled their drinks on me. *What morons!*"

Sarah raised an eyebrow, recalling that Claire was actually the one who spilled the drink. But she smiled. "Oh, I'm sure they didn't mean it. Accidents happen."

Claire finished cleaning up the wine stain and told Sarah, "UGH! I'm not even sure he is worth the trouble." She vacillated.

"Well, I suppose I could give him another chance," she declared, tugging downward on her already plunging neckline.

WTF? Is she checking to make sure they are still there?

Claire pursed her lips in the mirror and reapplied her lipstick, cranking up the wattage on her bimbo meter.

She handed Sarah the used wipe, and exited the ladies room as she muttered an insincere, "Thanks."

Sarah looked down at her hand. She tossed the packet into the trashcan on her way out of the ladies room. She muttered to herself

"Don't mention it."

Asswipe.

Alex spotted Sarah, walking back to her table. He became temporarily distracted. But he soon lost track of her as he turned his full attention to Claire.

Sarah sat down at the table. Mary was on her phone. She opened the menu and waited patiently for Mary to end her call. Placing her phone on the table, Mary apologized,

"Sorry. I'm just busy, busy, busy." She unfolded the papers again.

"Now, where were we? Oh, yes. I have outlined the minimum list of things you *absolutely have* to do before I can put the house on the market."

She showed Sarah the two-page list. Sarah rolled her eyes, but it was difficult to focus on what she was saying. Mary's voice became background noise as Sarah's eyes strayed over to the bar.

Sarah noticed that Alex's friends were beginning to leave. Before long, it looked like Alex was alone with Claire.

They continued with the conversation about the house throughout dinner. Their waitress had just presented them with their checks, when

Alex and Claire got up and walked away from the bar. As they made their way toward the door, he remembered that he had seen Sarah earlier. He glanced quickly to see if she was still there. He smiled.

Alex steered Claire over to Sarah's table, his arm around Claire. He grinned as his eyes met Sarah's. "Hey. I thought that was you. Isn't the food here great?"

Claire pouted. It was obvious that if she'd had a choice, they wouldn't be standing there. She tugged on Alex's arm.

Sarah gestured across the table toward Mary. "Alex, this is Mary, my real estate agent." Then, her eyes pointing at Claire, she asked, "And ...?"

Alex guffawed. "Oh, I'm sorry. Sarah - this is Claire. Claire - Sarah."

Sarah smiled but Claire did not reciprocate. She ignored Sarah completely.

Mary hastily handed Alex one of her cards. "If you have any Real Estate needs, I'm your *go-to* person."

He took her card "That's *some house*, isn't it?" Mary responded quickly, shaking her head.

"Oh, there's *nothing* I can't work with. By the time I am done, you won't even *recognize* the place!"

Alex gave Sarah a funny look. She nodded back at him, acknowledging that she knew that was not what he meant, but Mary was just in her own little world.

He turned to Claire, who was still in a state of agitation. It was obvious that she did not appreciate the attention Sarah was getting. She nudged Alex again, playing up to him.

Claire looked at Sarah and Mary with a controlled, teeth-clenched grin. "Sorry we have to leave so soon, but there's a bottle of Cabernet Sauvignon waiting for us, back at my place." She leaned into Alex, pawing him, speaking just over a whisper in his ear. "Shall we?"

What is the big deal with this guy anyway? What is so spectacular about Alex that Claire can't wait to be alone with him?

Sarah caught her eyes scanning, involuntarily examining his belt line ... then lower. She was overcome with a crimson red flush and she quickly looked back up to his face. She was certain the whole restaurant had followed the path her eyes had just been on.

The fact she was so aware of Alex's presence bothered Sarah. It made her uncomfortable. And what really made it worse was the way he looked back at her with cool, friendly disinterest. She caught herself in an involuntary attempt to increase the size of her breasts, as she compared herself to the "ample" Claire.

Alex put Mary's card in his jacket. He smiled at Sarah.

Sarah's heart was beating so hard in the confines of her ribs; she had to remind it to stay in its cage. Alex slowly backed away from the table, Claire taking the lead. He winked at Sarah as they turned to leave.

"Good seeing you again, Sarah." But he abruptly turned around before they reached the door and stepped back toward her.

"Hey - you know, the guys are giving me a little "going away" party, here. I want you to come." He thought for a moment as the details came to him. "It's on the 21st, the day before I leave, at 6:30."

Sarah looked unsure.

Alex coaxed her. "It would be a great way for you to meet some people."

She was doubtful.

"Come on. You'll have fun."

"Well, maybe …"

Alex grinned and pointed at Sarah as he backed out the door. "We'll see you there then. Be there!" He winked. "I mean it."

Alex and Claire stepped out onto the sidewalk. Sarah didn't turn her head, but she could see Claire, snuggling up to Alex, as they walked past the window.

~ THIRTEEN ~

THERE WERE TWO OTHER residents in the activity room, watching television. A nurse looked on as she made notes on a clipboard.

Alex was sitting at a small table, facing Irene. He pushed a small stack of papers across the table to her.

Irene put her glasses on. She adjusted them, sliding them down slightly on her nose. She lifted the top paper and studied the printed copy on the second page. Alex scanned her face for an indication of what she was thinking. He grinned.

"See? I told you that was one special car. I am *sure* we can get multiple offers, whenever you are ready to sell it."

Irene placed the top page back on the pile. She removed her glasses and gently placed them on the stack. She looked, intently, over at Alex. She felt a tearing in her heart.

"Alex, have you ever felt as if the timing just wasn't right?"

His smile flattened. He leaned forward, toward Irene, and rested his elbows on the table. "You really don't want to sell the car, do you?"

Irene looked softly at him. "I'm sorry, Alex. You have put so much time into all of this for me." She touched the papers again.

Alex sat back in the chair, a little puzzled. He leaned forward again, with compassion.

"It has to be your decision." He gave her reassuring smile." Don't worry about my time. I had fun doing it." He paused.

"But I'm curious. Why hold onto something that can't do anything for you?"

The nurse escorted the two other residents out of the room.

Irene's eyes searched around to see if they were alone. Then her eyes met his. She smiled feebly at Alex, and then she turned over her hands and stared at the lines.

"I just can't help feeling that there's another, more important purpose, out there waiting for it." She shifted her eyes back to his.

"Oh, I don't know. Maybe I really am just a crazy old lady, Alex."

The nurse returned and turned off the TV. She smiled at Irene as she approached. "Are you ready for dinner, Irene?"

Alex stood. He pulled out Irene's chair, assisting her to her feet. She leaned on him, for a moment. Alex noticed that she was struggling to keep her balance, making it almost impossible to walk. She stared at him with disappointment and a sad expression. He encouraged her to lean on him and they began walking slowly to the door.

At the main hallway, the nurse took Irene's arm and gently began to guide her toward the dining room. Alex released her arm and, as just as she reached the entrance to the dining room, he called out,

"If you change your mind, I will help you sell the car. Just let me know." He took out his keys from his pocket and followed with, "You take care, Irene."

Irene smiled back at him. "Goodbye sweetheart. Thank you for everything."

Alex pushed on the glass doors and stepped outside. The nurse turned to Irene.

"Isn't he just the nicest young man …and so handsome, too."

~ FOURTEEN ~

CHRISTMAS MUSIC WAS SOFTLY playing on the radio in the background.

After loosely tying the bib apron protecting her clothes, Sarah rolled up the sleeves of her shirt and swept two potholders from the counter. The door of the old Kenmore range opened and she removed a cookie sheet brimming with freshly baked cookies.

Sarah set it on the table and smiled. Soft-centered, but crisp around the edges, they waited in anticipation of how they would be decorated. She had just filled a pastry bag with icing, when her phone rang; she made a face and set the bag back on the counter.

"Hi Jess. Thanks for getting back to me so soon. I know you are busy with your family and stuff." Placing a hand on one hip, she added,

"Are you ready for this? I just took my first batch of cookies out of the oven. I memorized Irene's recipe, but I can't remember how to make your *Blizzard Blitz* icing. Mine is too sweet."

Sarah frowned. "You know Jess - this is the first time in 5 years that we haven't done this together. It feels strange." She listened intently as she received instructions from the other end.

A virtual light bulb went on in her head as it all came back to her. "Oh - So *that's* what I did wrong. What was I thinking? See? I really *do* need you"

She laughed. She frowned again. Then she giggled.

"No, I didn't forget the *most important part* of our tradition!"

Sarah removed a bottle from a paper bag. She held the bottle up to the light. She read the label aloud to Jess as she proudly placed the bottle next to the cooling cookie sheet.

"Pino Noir - from *New Zealand.*" She paused and then went on.

"I know. But Jess, you know it won't be the same." She smiled, and then laughed out loud.

"Don't worry. Yes, I *am* lonely, but I'm not going to down the *whole bottle*! *God Jess*!" She gathered new ingredients for the new batch of icing from the refrigerator.

"I hear Rodney in the background. Give him a hug for me. I will be home soon. We'll all get together and celebrate." She dumped the ingredients in the mixing bowl.

"I miss you too, sweetie. Bye."

Sarah placed the phone in the pocket of the apron. She pouted a little bit, and then walked toward the bottle of wine, studying it. She opened the drawer and took out a corkscrew.

Scouring through an upper cupboard, Sarah traded her coffee mug for a lone, stemmed wine glass. She sighed, rinsing it quickly, not knowing how long it had been since it had been put to good use.

Within a minute, there was a pause in the music. The kitchen was silent, except for the sound of the wine bottle being uncorked.

~ FIFTEEN ~

SARAH CRANKED UP THE VOLUME, gleefully singing upbeat Christmas songs along with the radio. She twirled while coating the cookies with *Blizzard Blitz*.

The re-capped wine bottle was about half empty. No longer protecting her shirt, by any stretch of the imagination, the tie on the neck of her apron had slipped even more, and had formed a complex knot.

Sarah was unaware that she had carelessly splattered cookie icing down the front of her blouse; there was a big glob on the tip of her nose.

Her attempt to decorate the cookies was quite comical - she laughed at what some of them looked like. She removed the first one from the pan. Sarah paused to look for the cookie bags she had bought earlier in the day.

There were at least 25 of them - they can't be lost already!"

She bopped off to the living room, where she remembered seeing the bags last, singing, wine bottle in her hand. Once she found them, she tucked them into the apron pockets for safekeeping, and headed back through the foyer.

Sarah heard a knock. She kept going, but she stopped as she passed the front door; there was another knock. Much louder than the first time, it was hard to ignore.

She opened the door. There was nobody there, so she closed it again. Before she had the chance to walk away, there was another knock. This time she heard distinct footsteps on the steps, outside. The door handle rattled. On her tiptoes, she comically sneaked up, grabbed the doorknob and hastily flung it open.

Setting her eyes upon a large tree branch on the bottom step of the landing, she chuckled, stepped out and down the steps to retrieve it. "Oh, no you don't. I'm not falling for that again!" Bottle still in her hand, Sarah bent over to pick up the branch.

A stiff breeze off the lake, danced around her, sweeping her apron up over her face, blocking her view. When she managed to get the apron back in place, she turned back to the door - just in time to see and hear it slam shut.

Again.

Sarah quickly set the wine bottle down beside the front step, in the bushes. She pounded on the door, anxiously trying to find a way to get back into the house by herself. She made the full circle around the house again, hoping to find something that would help. She'd just had the back window replaced; that was not an option.

Embarrassed, frustrated and, having had a little more spirits than she was used to in one sitting, Sarah reached in the pocket of her apron and took out her phone. She hesitated and put it back in the pocket.

Shit. I can't do that again!

Sarah shook her head, walking back to the driveway. Another sudden breeze off the lake intensified, whipping around her, snatching the empty bags from her pockets, and scattered them down the street. She started to chase after them, but her foot slid on an icy patch - she went down on one knee and watched the bags vanish completely.

Sarah returned to the front steps. She sat on the second step, shaking her head. She rested her head in her hands for a moment. She sighed out loud, yanked the phone from the apron pocket again and reluctantly placed a call to Alex.

~ SIXTEEN ~

ALEX AND CLAIRE WERE in his car, after dinner, on their way back to Claire's place. Claire pulled down the sun visor and looked at herself in the vanity mirror.

"I cannot *believe* you don't mind being seen in this old car. Don't you *worry* about what people think?"

Alex smiled and looked over at her. "I love driving this Mustang. There are only a few of these left, you know."

Claire muttered under her breath to herself, "Thank *God* for small favors." She flipped the visor up sharply and raised her voice. "Alex - *nobody* will ever take you seriously, if you don't step up your image - here in Cleveland or in Miami, you know."

He laughed at Claire's comment, not realizing she was dead serious.

She walked her fingers along his leg. "Not to worry … it's nothing that a little intervention can't take care of."

The conversation was interrupted by Alex's phone. Claire rolled her eyes.

Alex reached across to pick up the phone. "Hello?"

The worry in Sarah's voice was obvious as she answered him. "Alex - I am *really* sorry to bother you like this again. Please don't be mad."

He kept his tone calm, sensing she was in some kind of trouble. "Why would I be mad at you? … Sarah, are you *alright*?"

But she didn't answer. Alex could hear the gusty breeze in the background. "Where are you?"

She huffed and replied quietly. "I am sitting on the front step at the house, staring at a very big tree branch." Then she turned her head, inhaled deeply and spotted the partial bottle of wine she had stashed in the vegetation.

"Claire and I will be right there."

Claire rolled her eyes at the thought of seeing Sarah again.

Back on the front steps, Sarah tucked her phone back in the pocket of her apron. Reaching into the shrubbery, Sarah rescued the bottle. She rolled her eyes at the thought of seeing Claire again.

In anticipation of the impending encounter with Claire, Sarah uncorked the bottle. She raised it to her lips and tossed her head back. And the grape juice was history.

~ SEVENTEEN ~

ALEX'S CAR PULLED INTO the driveway. The lights abruptly dimmed.

Sarah was sitting quietly on the front steps. Embarrassed and cold, she hid behind her folded arms across her chest, painfully aware that her earlier decision, to leave her bra on the bathroom rack, was probably not a smart move. She felt very exposed and more than a little stupid.

She barely acknowledged Alex and the *lovely Claire* as they walked in her direction. She just stared at the dead spot in the air between them. Alex bent over and blinked at Sarah.

"Are you going to tell me *what's* going on now?"

A disgusted Claire tugged on Alex's arm and whispered aloud, "She doesn't look like she needs any help. Let's go home." Claire stared impatiently at her.

Sarah looked up at Alex.

Crap. Are they staring at me? I'll bet Claire is really enjoying the fact that I can't compete with her "dual mounds of magnificence."

Frustration building, Sarah released her arms, gesturing with her hands as she went into defense mode. Alex's eyes immediately shifted downward, to the paper-thin blouse, and what was obviously just underneath it.

Damn. Do not ogle... don't stare. He felt beads of sweat forming on the sides of his neck. *Who goes out in these temperatures dressed like that?*

Alex prided himself on *always* being prepared - for *everything*.

"I was talking to Jess and baking Christmas cookies. And somebody was knocking at the door," She explained.

Knowing that the *ever-so-responsible* Alex would be skeptical, she prepared a preemptive strike and quickly defended herself. "I *swear* - there *really was* a knock!"

He could have laughed, but he fought the urge. A smile twisted one corner of his lips. Alex struggled to keep from grinning. He put his hands on his hips. "Sarah - did you lock yourself out again?" he asked her in a mildly scolding manner.

Claire's phone rang, begging to be answered. She grabbed it from her purse and walked down the driveway, not stopping until she was at the sidewalk.

Alex walked silently to the side of the house. Sarah picked up the tree branch and followed him to the first patio door, where he was already preparing to break in. She stopped and tossed the branch into the bushes.

"Sort of. But, it wasn't like you think." Then, looking downward at her snow-covered shoes, she said, "I know you don't think I'm very smart."

He looked back at her with surprise. "Who said *that*?"

"You didn't *have* to say it."

Alex shook his head as he broke the bottom right pane in the door. He reached in and unlocked it. "You know ... whoever buys this place is really going to have to invest in a *damn good* security system."

The door opened and Alex quickly disappeared inside. He found himself in what appeared to be a bedroom - at least, underneath all of the paper and boxes, he thought there was probably a bed.

As he walked through the room, Alex was hit with the mouthwatering aroma of freshly baked cookies.

He shouted from the room, "Did you turn the oven off?" He didn't wait for her to answer. She hadn't displayed much responsibility in his eyes, up to this point.

Alex tore off through the house. Relieved that the oven was off, he stopped to admire the Christmas cookies Sarah had decorated. He laughed at the unique personalities she had given to some of them.

In the foyer, Alex hesitated by the table with a set of keys and stopped. He picked them up and took them with him. Alex unlocked and opened the front door.

Sarah had wandered back to the front of the house. She was sitting on the bottom step. Alex noticed the wine bottle that she had returned to the bushes. A little light bulb went off over his head.

Claire walked back up the driveway toward the house. As she approached the landing, she shot Sarah an arrogant look down the bridge of her nose. "Well, *good.* Now you are in, *aren't* you?" She turned to Alex. "There. She's fine. Now we can go home." She turned and started down the driveway to Alex's car.

But Alex called out to her, "I think we need to make sure she gets in okay. She's not exactly *herself* right now."

Claire couldn't have been less interested. Without even turning around, she said, "Be my guest. But I'm staying out here. I have work to do."

Alex moved down to Sarah's level and sat on the step, next to her. He picked up the bottle and examined it, noting that it was empty. He turned his head and studied Sarah. "Are you going to be OK?"

She faced him. "Why *wouldn't* I be?"

He tried to be discreet to prevent Claire from overhearing him. He showed Sarah the bottle in his hand. "How much did you have tonight?"

Sarah stood, and abruptly bolted up the steps. She stopped on the stoop and shot him a dirty look. "It was a *special occasion*! And it wasn't *that* much!"

She grabbed the door handle in an attempt to make a hasty, dramatic exit, but it was locked. She held her fingertips to the icy glass. She was flustered. Sarah pressed her forehead against the cold front door, in defeat.

What a dumb shit. Can't even make a smooth exit.

Alex joined her, the soft metallic jingling sounds coming from the pocket of his jacket as he reached the landing. He grinned and held out the keys to her.

"It helps if you have these." He inserted the key in the lock and it opened effortlessly.

Sarah hastily stepped into the foyer and made a weak attempt to close the door. Alex stuck out his hand, stopping it and quickly jumped in behind her.

As he shut the door, she turned to him, losing her balance slightly, knocking a vase off the table. Alex quickly reached out and caught it before it hit the floor. He returned the vase to the tabletop and breathed a sigh of relief. "I think you need to go to bed and sleep this off."

Sarah responded with a renewed sense of spirit. "I can't. I have more cookies to bake." She scurried off to the kitchen. Alex dashed quickly after her.

Sarah picked up a particularly funny-looking cookie and brought it over to Alex. She moved in closer and held it up to his face.

When she lost her balance again, momentarily leaning into him, his eyes were reminded, once again, what was standing at attention through the fragile fabric of her blouse.

Jesus. Stop staring at her breasts.

He considered stepping back a little - but he didn't. However, she did, with a devilish grin on her face.

Sarah playfully attempted to coax him to open his mouth. "Here. This one is *yours*. It even *looks* like you. Open up."

Not interested in a cookie at the moment, Alex grabbed the cookie from Sarah's hand and started to place it back on the table. She looked at him as if she was going to cry.

God, she is such a complicated woman! What a strange combination of softness and stubbornness.

She intrigued him. But that was all - nothing else. He quickly took a bite of the cookie and smiled, trying his best to humor her. He nodded at her. "Thank you. It's good."

She took the cookie from his hand, crinkled her nose at him disapprovingly and quietly mouthed, "Just good?"

*Crap. **Now** what did I do wrong?*

He thought briefly, and then he told her with a crooked smile, "Sarah - this is the *best* cookie I have *ever* had."

Her eyes flashed as she asked him in a tiny voice, "… *Ever*?"

"Yes, Sarah, *ever!*"

She is confusing the hell out of me.

Sarah's eyelids were beginning to droop. Alex gently guided her out of the kitchen. He turned out the light. They were back in the foyer.

She was falling asleep on her feet. He looked around for a place he could safely leave her for the night. The living room sofa was out of the question. It was covered with boxes and bags. And the bedroom off the patio was a potential death trap, with all the clutter.

Alex glanced up the stairs. "I think we'd better get you up to bed, while you can still walk." He paused.

*How many times would **that** line have come in handy over the last few years?*

Alex quickly searched the hallway for Sarah.

Facing the stairs by herself was a more daunting task than she had anticipated. She stopped three times to keep herself from taking a tumble. Sarah continued up the stairs. She turned out the stairway lights.

Alex switched them back on so he could see where he was going. She turned them off again. Alex switched them back on, shaking his head. He was amused.

Stumbling over a box on the floor, Sarah boogied into the bedroom singing "*Jingle Bells.*" She leaned over and turned on a lamp by the bed.

She whispered, "*Shhh* - don't tell anybody I sleep with this light on. I'm just a big old *scaredy-cat.*" She made a funny face at him, pretending she had whiskers, and then grinned. She moved over to the window.

Alex pulled the covers back on the bed. He pointed to Sarah. She hesitated. "It's too *early* to go to bed!" she whined from across the room, beginning to retreat to the window.

Nice try, but I have the obvious advantage here. Stop being so difficult – I am trying to help you.

He managed to pin Sarah in one place and reached around her waist to untie her apron. He untangled the knot behind her neck, trying not to pull her hair, which had fallen out of her clip.

Sarah reeled. *Please ... Don't feel good on my neck. Don't make me feel drowsy ... don't make me feel all warm inside.*

Alex felt her whole body relax into his arms, telling him that she trusted him completely. It was a nice feeling.

He chuckled as he tossed the tangled apron onto a chair. "I would hate to have you choke yourself during the night in this thing." He steered her closer to the bed, where she fell back flat, staring up at the ceiling.

There was an unmistakable lack of self-consciousness about her that Alex hadn't seen before, that brought light to her face. He sat beside her and he slipped off her shoes.

She popped up into a sitting position, with a big grin. "Guess what?"

Alex was a little startled. He looked back at her. "What?"

Sarah gave him a wide-eyed look of bewilderment, not remembering that she had asked him the question. "*What* what?"

Alex shook his head and nudged her gently, back onto the bed.

She smiled at him innocently, completely unaware that three of the buttons on her blouse had popped open, exposing her breasts in all of their nakedness and glory. As they taunted him, it took every bit of restraint he possessed to keep his eyes from wandering to them.

Shit. Should I button the shirt for her? Or would that just make things worse and come off looking like I am copping a friggin' feel?

Alex's hands immediately stilled. He leaned into her space and covered her with the blanket. Tunneling his fingers through his hair, he felt a flash of guilt for what he found himself thinking.

Within minutes, she looked like she had fallen asleep. He reached to turn the lamp off, but his eyes rested on her again.

He disappeared into the bathroom. The sound of water followed. Alex returned to Sarah's bedside with a damp washcloth. He observed her for a moment.

He leaned over the bed and gently wiped the icing off her nose. She sighed in her sleep. Alex moved in closer to dissolve the last of the sugary glaze. Just as he was wiping off the last little bit, Sarah's eyes popped open.

She shot up, the fire suddenly back in her eyes, and she met him, nose-to-nose. "Did anybody ever tell you that you are *insanely cute*, when you want to be?"

Alex was surprised. He felt himself flush slightly. He smiled back at her. "No ... not lately." He paused, and then he continued. "Okay, Sarah ... I think it's time for you to ..."

Sarah grabbed Alex by the collar of his jacket and pulled him in, giving him a fiery, passionate kiss. He was caught off-guard and lost his balance as he tried not to fall on her. His black leather gloves tumbled out of his pocket onto the blanket.

Alex found himself on the bed, propped up on his elbows, eye-to-eye with Sarah. He studied her. He pulled back; his lips were still tingling from the passion of her wet kiss.

An unrepentant grin flashed across her face. Then her smile turned upside-down, into a frown. "Sorry - *bad* idea?" She brushed her hair back out of her lazy eyes. "... *too impulsive* - you are *right*. I am just *too* damn *impulsive!*" She found his hand, and her thumbs brushed across his knuckles. "Were you at least a *little* ... you know ... *aroused?*"

A slight pink traveled up from Alex's neck, meeting his cheeks. His brows drew together, and the corners of his mouth lifted in a bemused smile.

How the shit am I supposed to answer that?

He sat up on the edge of the bed again, at a loss for words. He glanced away. Quickly turning back to her, he said, "Listen, Sarah - you're not yourself tonight. You're not going to remember any of this ..."

Alex stopped in mid-sentence. The silence in the room had been interrupted by the faint sound of snoring. Sarah was sound asleep.

He smirked. "... and I rest my case." Alex tucked the blanket up around her, unknowingly hiding his gloves well under the blanket.

Sarah smiled in her sleep, pulling the blanket around her face. She turned on her side. He walked to the door and turned off the light on the way out.

But he quickly made a U-turn, returning to the room, and he turned the lamp back on.

He was smiling.

~ ~ ~ ~ ~

Claire was waiting in the car. Still on the phone, she didn't even realize he had been gone more than a minute or two. She ended her call when Alex opened the car door. Silence enveloped them as they backed out of the driveway.

After about two minutes, Alex turned to Claire. "Sorry it took so long. She was really out of it. I don't know what happened to her tonight. I think she's really missing her friends back home. I was afraid she might fall down those stairs."

Under her breath, Claire seethed. "We should *be* so lucky."

Alex looked past the steering wheel at her. "Sorry - I couldn't hear you. What did you say?"

As they passed the entrance to the park, she quickly saved herself. "I said she was *lucky* we stopped by."

~ EIGHTEEN ~

SARAH WAS ON HER phone, dragging clothing out of the closet and her suitcase. She became more frustrated with each piece she looked at, holding them up, imagining what she would look like in the mirror. She dramatically articulated an introduction, in a different character voice, describing how she thought she looked in them.

Holding a plain, navy blue sweater in front of her, she said, "Hello - I'm *"Boring."*

She tried on a baggy sweatshirt. "Hi - I'm *"Frumpy."*

She made a face and tore the sweatshirt off, replacing it with a clingy, silk blouse. "Good evening. My name is *Claire*," she said, turning up her nose.

Exasperated, she ripped the blouse off, and pulled a tight, red sweater over her head. She exaggerated the plunging neckline as she spoke. "And ... I'm a ... *slut.*"

Sarah frowned at herself in the mirror. Her phone interrupted the fashion session. It was Jess. She smiled and answered, standing in front of the mirror, wearing only her pink silk bra and panties. She grimaced as she silently pointed out the flaws staring back at her.

"I'm telling you, Jess - I don't remember much about that night, after I talked to you." She moved her phone to the other ear and continued to study herself in the mirror. "I remember I had to call for help getting back into the house, but after that - just little bits and pieces that don't make any sense."

She noticed a bump under the blanket on the bed. She reached over to smooth it out with her hand, but it didn't flatten out. Sarah pulled back the blanket. She jerked backward and froze, as two black leather gloves revealed themselves to her, mixed in with the sheets and blanket on the bed. She gasped.

"Oh my God, Jess! There's a pair of men's gloves in my bed, under the blanket!" she shrieked in horror. Panic set in as fragmented images of Alex's face flung themselves at her.

What did she do?

"Do you think I *could* have?" She pulled the gloves out and put them on top of the blanket. "... or *would* have?"

Sarah was absolutely mortified. "Oh, Jess - I *can't* go to this party now! In fact, I can *never* show my face again!" She struggled to remain calm as she received long distance moral support from Jess. "You're right. There has to be a reasonable explanation for this." She sat on the bed with the gloves in her hand,

The only thing worse than having a one-night-stand, was not remembering if you'd had one or not. Sarah lay there with the gloves, staring up at the ceiling.

Then she crashed back, and closed her eyes.

~ NINETEEN ~

THE ESTABLISHMENT WAS a noisy, lively place - perfect for a going-away party. Talking and laughter filled the air. The comforting clatter spilled out from the bar, drawing Sarah in.

One of Alex's friends, Rick, noticed Sarah immediately. He quickly jumped up from his table and held the door for her. Sarah felt out of place.

"Please tell me you're here for Alex's party. I'd hate to think I'll never see you again." He winked at her, gesturing to help her take off her coat. He definitely needed a closer look at her.

Sarah removed her coat, revealing a rather conservative heather-gray ski sweater. However, that only served as a sharp contrast to the tight, form-fitting charcoal pencil skirt that ended about 10 inches above her knees.

Back at the house, she had wondered if the skirt might not be appropriate for this party. If the general reaction was any indication, it clearly was not a problem.

"Alex was the first person I met in Cleveland. I'm still sort of new in town."

Rick took her coat. "We'll take care of you."

Sarah paused and looked at the table. Every guy there was either holding a cell phone or had one on the table in front of him.

Ooh ... guys with tools ... could it get any geekier than this?

Actually, she was impressed that they were so friendly - such a refreshing change from some of the pompous asses she had spent time with in the past. They made her laugh. And they were happy to have her join them.

She noticed Claire, at the bar, with Alex, but she quickly looked away.

Rick joined them at the table, with a beer for Sarah. She took a drink from the bottle and smiled at him. Hearing his friends laughing, Alex glanced across the room and saw that they were with Sarah.

Alex watched Sarah, from the bar, as she interacted with his friends. He caught her eye and they exchanged a quick smile. Claire walked away with one of his friends, laughing flirtatiously, as Alex approached Sarah's table.

Rick stood and proclaimed, "And here's the man of the evening!" Applause erupted throughout the bar. Alex grinned and waited for things to quieten down.

Amused, Alex pointed to the beer in front of Sarah and teased her. *"What?* No wine tonight?"

Sarah was sure she turned at least a thousand shades of red. She couldn't look at him.

What had really happened that night? She didn't know how much of what she was recalling actually happened, and how much she imagined, compliments of the alcohol. She wasn't even sure the gloves belonged to Alex.

Alex pulled out a chair across from Sarah and joined his friends. Rick leaned in and spoke. "Dude - just think - in a couple of weeks, while we are all fighting the ice and snow in Cleveland, you will be sitting in a bar, surrounded by dozens of *hot, scantily dressed babes.*

He hesitated for only a few seconds, then playfully grasped Alex by the front of his shirt, begging him, *"Please* take me with you!" The plea was followed by laughter at the table.

Sarah took a few more sips of her beer. "Be careful what you wish for."

Alex looked at Sarah, remembering that her grandmother had used that same line on him. "What's that supposed to mean?"

She giggled as the beer caught up with her. "I'm not sure. It's just something my grandmother has always said. Probably because she couldn't think of anything else to say."

Rick leaned over, behind Sarah's chair. He rubbed her shoulders. "So, Alex, where have you been hiding Sarah all this time?" He squeezed her arm. "Well, I'm just glad you are leaving her behind."

Sarah laughed, gently prying Rick's hands away from her and diplomatically told him, "*Nobody* leaves *me* behind." She paused, realizing that she had never said anything so self-confident before. She liked it. "I am going back home in a few days."

The others at the table showed interest in her background. Alex enthusiastically filled them in. "Sarah is a voice-over artist in New York. She is the voice of ..." He looked to Sarah for help.

Smiling, surprised and impressed that he remembered that much, she helped him out. "I am *Princess Penelope* - of the planet *Proton*."

Alex's friends jokingly stood, bowing before Sarah. She laughed.

Before long, appetizers appeared at the bar. Alex's friends and Sarah migrated and filled their plates.

Alex didn't return to the table; he joined another group of his friends at the bar.

Sarah was the first to return to the table, plate of food in her hand. She sat and looked around. She finished her beer. Rick joined her, with two more bottles. He placed them on the table and sat next to her. Their knees brushed under the table.

When the DJ began to play Christmas music, the people at the table slowly scattered around to other tables, and the dance floor began populating. Sarah found herself at the table, alone.

Alex, noticing that Sarah was by herself, walked his beer over to the table. He pulled up a chair, turned it backwards and straddled it, and he faced her. As the classic Nat King Cole version of *The Christmas Song* played, he tossed back his beer and set the empty bottle on the table.

Claire, from across the room, made note of Sarah, at the table with Alex, but she remained at a safe distance.

"So, where are things with the house?"

Sarah shrugged her shoulders. "Where do I start?"

The song continued. Sarah lost herself in the lyrics. Quietly singing to herself, she whispered, "*Everybody knows - a turkey and some mistletoe - helps to make the season bright ...*"

She leaned in and told Alex, "This is my all-time-favorite Christmas song. My Grandfather used to dance with me in the living room. He played the scratchy old record on his stereo. But we never heard the scratches - just the music."

"I remember my mom playing that record at the holidays too. That guy singing has got to be older then dirt."

"He's dead."

Of course he is, you shithead. What the hell is wrong with you?

Alex grinned and stood. He extended his hand out to Sarah. "Not to be outdone by your grandfather … would you like to …"

But before Alex could ask Sarah for the dance, Claire appeared from out of the shadows and latched onto his arm. "Alex, you wouldn't say no to *me* for *one last, little dance*, would you?"

Alex shook his head and glanced back at Sarah. "Um … Claire - we were just about to …"

"No, *no*. Go on." Sarah smiled and nudged him. "You two go on. I'll be fine. I'm just enjoying the music."

Claire and her long-legged strides swept Alex away to the opposite side of the dance floor.

Screw you, Claire.

Rick approached Sarah and, feeling like she really didn't have a choice, she reluctantly followed him onto the dance floor.

Throughout the song, Alex scanned over and watched Sarah with Rick. He held her tight, and Alex couldn't help noticing his hands, to Sarah's chagrin, moving to her buttocks on more than one occasion.

Simultaneously, Sarah focused on Alex with the ever-clingy Claire, but neither noticed the other at the same time.

~ TWENTY ~

ALEX COMBED THROUGH THE parking lot, thanking everybody as they walked to their cars. Claire disappeared, gabbing on her phone, only to resurface when she sensed Alex moving in Sarah's direction.

Sarah was at her car. Rick walked past her and called out to Alex. "Hey Alex! Sarah's leaving!"

The cold wind picked up. Alex pulled his scarf up around his neck and placed his hands in his pockets. He approached Sarah and he grinned. She smiled back at him.

"... So ... this is it, huh?" He took his cold hands from his pockets and held out his arms to give her a good-bye hug. She went to him.

Alex lingered. He smiled and brushed the tiny snowflakes off her face. "You take care of yourself."

"You too."

Alex and Sarah pulled back and smiled again. They shared a quick, awkward kiss, just as Claire joined them. It was a tiny kiss, but it was enough to send adrenaline shooting through him.

"You will have to visit us in Miami someday," Claire addressed Sarah, in a voice dripping with sarcasm.

Sarah gave Alex a puzzled look. But before Alex could say anything, Claire finished her message. She chirped, "We realized that the complex my condo in Miami is in, is the *same one* Alex is moving to. Of course, I only get down there once a month. But, *what a coincidence!*"

Sarah smiled. "Imagine that."

Claire pulled Alex away. He touched Sarah's arm as he retreated with her.

Once he and Claire were at the Mustang, he waved one last time, calling out, "Hey - Good luck with the house! Tell Irene goodbye for me."

As Claire got into the car, she said to Alex, "Honestly. I cannot *believe* you *lost* your gloves! *Well*, it doesn't matter, does it? You won't need them anymore."

"Who's *Irene?*"

~ TWENTY-ONE ~

IT WAS RAINING outside. Sarah was carefully adorning the Christmas tree with vintage glass ornaments and trinkets from her grandparents' boxes that she and Alex had recently uncovered in the garage attic.

Not expecting company, she was dressed casually, in faded jeans and a soft pink sweater that took turns sliding off her shoulders, her hair carelessly falling down in loose waves.

Sarah studied each ornament before hanging it in just the right place. She walked to the light switch and flipped it off. The room came alive with the lights and ornaments glistening on the tree. A huge grin spread from ear to ear as Sarah placed the last ornament on the tree.

The doorbell rang.

Curious as to who it could be, Sarah slowly made her way through the foyer to the front door. She was surprised to find Alex, standing there, in the porch light.

"Hey; come on in out of the rain."

Alex laughed as he stepped inside. "Yeah; welcome to Cleveland."

Sarah closed the door behind him. "I thought you would have been long gone by now."

Alex removed his jacket and shook the water off. He continued into the foyer.

There was an air of distant preoccupation about him, as if he wasn't exactly sure why he was there himself. He ran his hand through his hair, wet from the rain.

He looked like he was at war with himself. "Um, I just wanted to stop by to say goodbye again and …," he pulled out the keychain with the house keys on it from his pants pocket. "... To return these to you." He held the keys out to her.

Sarah grinned, playfully pushing them back to him. "I might lock myself out again." She giggled. *"Who'll rescue* me?" But her smile quickly faded with the realization that Alex wouldn't be able to rescue her, long distance. She tossed the keys on the table.

The keychain slid across the surface and rested, hanging over the edge, by the chair with Alex's jacket. As she walked away, the keys wavered, then fell onto the jacket.

Christmas music from the living room filled the air in the background. Moonlight spilled through the window, dancing across the floor, illuminating its polished, hardwood surface. He walked to the window and studied his own reflection staring in at him from outside. He turned back to the living room.

Alex's eyes locked in on the Christmas tree, as he gently handled an ornament. "Are these the old ones we found in the crates?"

Sarah joined him at the tree. "They are beautiful, aren't they? They should never have been buried in dusty old boxes where they can't shine."

Alex began to lower himself into a chair, when the radio began playing an updated version, of *"The Christmas Song."*

Remembering that this was the song Sarah liked, he quickly stood again with a smile, and held his hand out to Sarah. "There's that song again. I think I still owe you a dance."

Sarah grinned and took Alex's hand. They began to sway, holding each other close, both carefully avoiding eye contact. The heat between them was unmistakable as their bodies melded together to the sultry melody.

She felt safe. His nearness sent little shivers of awareness down her spine. Sarah wished time would stop and she could stay in the moment forever.

Alex was swept up in her fragrance. He struggled to stay focused. A powerful energy increased as their faces drew closer and closer, lips brushing slightly.

The song drew to an end. Their eyes met and locked. They were only a breath apart. And that was when Alex realized he was sunk.

Because Sarah Grayson was stealing his heart, one step, one *exasperating* breath at a time.

Jesus. What the hell is this?

Alex never had to struggle for control before. Because he *never lost* it in the first place.

Sarah studied his face. Something was different. She couldn't help noticing that the twinkle in Alex's eyes had been replaced by a deep, almost melancholy gaze. She wondered what he was thinking.

Alex let his hands wander lower, to Sarah's waist, pulled back, then to her face, fighting his urges. He slowly leaned in and his hands caressed the back of her neck. She went willingly, closing that fraction of an inch separating them. His mouth found hers, and there was an air of calmness as he kissed her, softly at first, then hesitated. The moment stretched between them.

He wanted to say something, but no words came out. He was completely lost in Sarah's eyes, and he kissed her again. Alex moved in closer, for just a moment and then pulled away; once again breaking the contact between them.

But the sizzle remained.

Before they knew it, the kiss they were sharing had evolved into uncontrollable passion. Alex couldn't keep his hands off her. Sarah felt her knees go weak. His brain struggled to keep up with what his body was doing.

God! What the hell is happening?

What was he doing? Alex had never been the *touchy-feely* type - pretty matter-of-fact about just about everything. And most of the time that seemed to work against him, especially with the ladies when it came to sex.

This was different. They were on the sofa. Then he had her on her back, on the floor. Dropping over Sarah, Alex planted his hands on either side of her, on the rug. He stopped and lowered his gaze, staring at her, hard, relentless and direct.

Alex's name fell from Sarah's lips as he let his mouth roam over the rise beneath her sweater, slowly finding his way down toward her belly button. Sarah was so lost in the sensation of his mouth on her skin that she barely noticed he had unbuttoned her jeans, and the zipper was down.

He ran his fingers along the row of lace peeking out from under where the zipper ended.

Alex stared at Sarah and whispered, "You are so damn beautiful."

Everything about his touch was just right. Alex caressed her curves and brushed his thumbs over her pebbling nipples. Heat burned everywhere he touched, and Sarah's lower half melted.

Running her fingers under his sweater, Sarah felt the muscles in Alex's back tense each time he touched her. He sucked in a breath as she rose upward against him. He paused slightly, yanking his own sweater and t-shirt off, revealing the results of all the afternoons he had spent working out.

Sarah had only a few seconds to take in the view before Alex had plastered himself on her again, this time with nothing from the waist up separating them. She grabbed his butt, to maintain a connection, pulling him closer. Her heart felt like it was expanding in her chest, and if it didn't stop, it would burst.

Sarah flipped over on top of him. Alex, never missing a beat, continued to clamp his mouth over hers in a deep kiss that was blazing with desire.

He flipped her back again. He caught her bottom lip gently between his teeth, then slowly released it, letting it slide free. A helpless whimper shook her chest as a fever rolled up her spine.

In the short time since they'd met, Alex knew this was not like any relationship he had ever been in before, but he never imagined it was anything like this.

She was irritating and irresistible at the same time. Was that even possible? Sarah made him uneasy yet comfortable, simultaneously. So damn comfortable that he forgot why he had come by in the first place.

And time stopped. Alex found himself smiling and he quickly wished he hadn't. Her spell wasn't going to work on him; he had plans – big ones. And they didn't include Sarah … or Cleveland. He caught himself falling.

What the hell are you doing, Wagner? Focus!

His hand slid out from underneath her. He quickly pulled her arms from around his neck and rolled off her onto the cold floor. He jumped up and bent over, rubbing his hands over his face.

Sarah sat up, a hank of her tousled hair dropping across her face. She bit her lower lip. He could see the tears forming in the outer corners of her eyes, waiting to be set free as she rolled her sweater back down and stood on wobbly legs. Sarah lifted her gaze as Alex whipped his head around to look at her.

Trembling, Alex firmly grasped both of her hands in his. With desperation in his voice, he swallowed and said, "No. This is a mistake!" He turned away and back again, his voice louder. He did not like not being in absolute control of his emotions. He swallowed again, only harder. "I've spent my *entire life* preparing for this; it's the path I have been on since I was still in school. I *have* to follow it. None of *this* is part of the plan."

Sarah smiled weakly, nodding that she understood. Still, tears continued welling in her eyes.

Alex stood and pulled his sweater back on over his head. He placed his hands on Sarah's shoulders. "I want you to go back home as soon as you can and go after your *own* dream. You deserve it! You are *so* bright and ... creative!"

He'd meant it as a compliment of sorts, but obviously, she had taken it differently than he'd intended. Alex continued digging the hole.

"Sarah ... we are *worlds apart*. I *never* should have stopped by like this again."

Sarah's mind replayed his comment and, wounded, she stiffened up, pulling away from Alex.

Worlds apart? ... Excuse me? What the hell is that supposed to mean?

No. She would not let another man tell her she wasn't good enough. A fire suddenly blazed in Sarah. She met his eyes with hers again. And she shot back at him.

The words sprang from her lips before she could call them back. "**You're right**. We *are* worlds apart. You should follow that *path* you have created for yourself, in your *pre-calculated, predictable* little life!"

He flinched, feeling like the blow came out of nowhere. Sarah's words struck Alex like a hammer. He suddenly felt like someone had just slugged him. He was surprised at her criticism, calling his life *pre-calculated*.

And she called him *predictable*. His stomach turned.

When the hell did this turn into a fight?

Alex always went out of his way to avoid fights. The only kind he liked were those he knew he would win. And this wasn't shaping up to be one of them.

Feeling the sting of hurt, he slowly backed away and out to the hall, toward the front door, to leave. He hastily grabbed his jacket from the chair.

Sarah followed him. When he reached the door, Alex turned back to her and gave her a forced smile.

She apologized. "Alex, I shouldn't have said that. I'm sorry. I didn't mean it. I *really do* want you to be happy."

He touched her elbow. "No, you're absolutely right. I *am* predictable. But that's just the way I am. It's in my make-up." He ran his fingers over the top of his head, combing through his hair in frustration. "I don't know how to be any other way."

Alex stepped outside and turned back to Sarah. The windy air tasted of frigid rain. "I want you to be happy too." He took her face in his hands. "You deserve somebody who believes in forever."

She forced her lips into a smile.

"Go back home to New York and turn that city upside down." He kissed her quickly. "And don't take any bullshit from anybody!" "Goodbye Sarah. Good luck."

Sarah's eyes glistened as the door closed behind him.

~ TWENTY-TWO ~

SARAH WALKED BACK INTO the living room. She moved a box, clearing a path to the tree. Raindrops dribbled down the window, obscuring the view outside of the Cleveland skyline. Sarah began opening the flaps on the box.

She reached inside and picked up an old photo album. She ran her fingers over the leather cover, almost afraid to touch the fragile pages inside.

Sarah took the book with her and found a spot in the window seat, silhouetted by the lonely lights of the Christmas tree. She leaned back and began leafing through the album. She felt as though she was browsing through a window of time.

The first was a faded black and white photograph featuring a young woman, in her twenties. It was summertime and she was standing outside in the front yard of the house. The woman was turning back, looking over her shoulder with a carefree smile, her dark locks shining in the sunlight. She certainly was a beauty.

It was Irene.

Sarah immersed herself in the memories of the endless starlit skies of her own summers spent at Edgewater and the sweet scent of new growth exploding from the rich earth. And the house - it possessed such a feeling of anticipation and hope.

The next was a larger image of a young couple, taken on the same day. Sarah was struck by the look on the man's face. There was such an unmistakable look of admiration on her grandfather's face. His eyes were obviously trained on Irene.

Love Light. That's what grandfather called it.

As Sarah studied the photographs, she found herself further lost in the fairy-tale. She wondered if she would ever experience that kind of love. She struggled to recall the early years, when her own parents actually loved each other.

Time and seasons change, and so did the chapters in the album.

Irene must have been in her early fifties. She was kneeling in a snow bank with her arms around a toddler. It was Sarah. She remembered seeing similar photos before, but not this exact picture. However, she did remember the next chapter.

Sarah was captivated by the montage featuring Sarah and both of her grandparents, playing in the snow covered front yard of the old house. She smiled as the recollection drifted back to her.

It was a frosty afternoon and her parents had dropped her off at the house for the weekend. Sarah couldn't have been older than nine or ten. Her grandfather's best friend and protégée, Nick, had just been promoted and had received a new camera as a gift. He couldn't wait to begin his new hobby. She closed her eyes and tried to remember what Nick looked like.

Sandy hair, steel-blue eyes that cut through you like a knife.

She remembered him as a big man, but that could have just been because she was so young at the time. But even if he really had been *larger than life,* as her grandfather had teased him, everybody knew he had a heart of pure gold. And he had a soft spot for kids.

Sarah recalled asking Irene if Nick had any children. She remembered thinking he was so much fun and would be a great dad.

All Irene would tell her was that some people just cannot have children, and that he was thinking about adoption one day.

Later, Sarah learned that Nick never realized his dream of becoming a dad, completely immersing himself in his career instead.

She paused to wonder why. Then she continued to turn the pages.

Her grandfather was the absolute best at building snowmen and taught her the fine art at an early age. He insisted there was a secret physics to it and, although Irene could be spotted in the background of the photographs, lovingly *sabotaging the structural integrity,* his snowmen seemed to be blessed with a mysterious longevity that was unique to them.

Sarah stopped and froze as she turned to the next page.

Snow angels. Oh my God! I haven't thought about those since these pictures were taken.

Sarah felt a tingling rush to her fingertips and toes, as if she was back there with them, lying in the snow, flapping her arms and legs in the ongoing contest to see who could make the best snow angel.

But the real challenge was to see which artist could get up and walk away from the creation leaving behind the least number of telltale footprints, embossed in the snow.

Irene was a great storyteller. She always wanted to be a writer, but life just seemed to get in the way. She loved holidays, music, melodies and everything that went along with them. Each Christmas Eve, she took great delight in sharing a new holiday story with family and friends.

Sarah gently closed the storybook, hugging it to her chest. She closed her eyes tight. Her lower lip jutted out as her thoughts wandered to the events over the past month, with Alex.

Although it was over, Sarah had to admit that if she had the chance to do it over, she wouldn't change meeting Alex.

Alex had been a missing link in her chain. Sarah had been wondering if she had missed something in life. Something like passion ... and *sizzle*. She definitely had found sizzle with Alex.

But even though she had found the passion that had been missing, she had to face the fact that it had gone away as suddenly as it had appeared. Maybe that was just the way it was meant to be.

The haves and the have-nots. Bullshit.

Sarah stood and placed the photo album on the window seat and gazed out at the framed skyline again.

~ ~ ~ ~ ~

Driving southbound in the hammering rain, Alex was quickly losing himself, deep in thought. As signs promising him of his long-awaited dream passed him, mixed in with the rhythm of the windshield wipers, he struggled to concentrate on the task at hand. He shook his head.

Rain continued to blow in windy sheets across the window. He shifted in his seat and repositioned his hands on the wheel.

*There's no way I could **ever** stay in Cleveland.*

Alex's hands moved on the steering wheel automatically. Lights from the oncoming cars flashed in his eyes as his thoughts drifted and he began driving on autopilot.

Subtle hints and images crept into his peripheral vision, reminding him that it was only hours before Christmas Eve.

He drove through a small town main street, strung with glistening lights. Sarah loved Christmas lights. She had a scatter-brained way about her. But maybe that just meant she needed somebody to help her navigate life safely.

There was something sweet, vulnerable, and fun about everything she said and did; even when Alex thought she was too impulsive.

Impulsive. Yeah, there was that.

The windshield was beginning to reflect a significant drop in the temperature outside, slowly transforming the cold rain from a wet drizzle to a slushy mess, accumulating as the wipers bullied it, pushing it around from side to side.

Miami had balmy evenings and tropical breezes … women with little more than underwear on …

But …

Sarah was powerfully erotic just by being herself, regardless of what she was wearing. She had no idea how stimulating she was. And that was just damn electrifying to Alex. The touch of her fingers on his body had been as gentle as a feather yet carried an impact that still shook him.

Miami held the promise of a new career, and the money to go along with it.

Alex's brain replayed the recollection of Sarah's scent, her hair, the softness of her skin. He struggled again to regain control. He grabbed the wheel again; one of the few things he still felt confident about having some kind of control over.

*Focus, focus, **focus**, Wagner … this is not like you.*

His mind came undone; everything started to unravel.

Wanting Sarah was a weakness. A terrible weakness that had been eating away at him one second, one minute, one hour at a time, over the past weeks - ever since she had invaded his life.

Florida had beaches and palm trees, and year round warm temperatures … and Claire would be there often …

Cleveland had his family and friends, and …

*... **Black ice ... HOLY SHIT!!!***

Alex's Mustang skidded sideways before performing a slow-motion spin. His life flashed before his eyes. He thought about everything; his childhood Christmas memories, his brother and family ... the night he learned his parents had been in that horrible accident ... the evening he met Sarah ...

He hit the brakes so hard he thought his foot would go right through the floorboards. The last thing on his mind was the look on Sarah's face as he left her just hours ago. It was burned into his brain.

There was a sudden jolt as his car halted, just inches short of the guardrail, foiling a steep plummet into the snow-covered rocky valley below.

Alex's pounding, suddenly heavy heart, dropped to his lap. He rubbed his hand over his face. He was tired. And, he had to admit - just a little bit scared.

Damn! That was close.

His fingertips brushed over his steering wheel, as he rested his forehead against the leather cover he had so carefully laced into place just a week before.

Alex straightened up in his seat, his brain completely void of any socially significant thoughts. His eyes caught a glimpse of a sign on the side of the old highway, just to the right of his front passenger fender. By the twisted, dented condition of the sign, it apparently had played a significant role in keeping his old Mustang on the road.

Alex opened the car door and stepped out to have a look at the damage. But not before his eyes settled onto the face of the sign. The hair on the back of his neck stood on end.

It was shaping up more and more like a bad 1960's Science Fiction movie. His face was granite. Alex raked his hand through his hair.

That can't be right. Cleveland – 200 Miles?

Through the twinkling lights of the oncoming traffic, Alex was finally able to clear his head and get his bearings straight.

He had spun completely around, crossing the 4-lane highway, and was resting against the northbound traffic sign, touting Cleveland was a mere 200 miles away.

No shit, Sherlock. 200 miles... in the wrong direction.

~ ~ ~ ~ ~

Sarah was still in the living room. She set the photo album carefully in the top of a box and folded the flaps in to protect it. Her thoughts were interrupted by her phone. Sarah hesitated as the ringer told her that Brad was calling. She stared down at the phone as it nagged at her.

How many times had she ignored his calls over the past month?

Finally, she answered it as she continued to scan the Cleveland lakefront, out the window. A long pause followed. "I've missed you too." She smiled weakly and stood. She walked to the doorway into the hall. "I would love to have dinner with you tomorrow night,"

Sarah took a last look around and turned off the lights on her way out of the living room - first the Christmas lights, and then the entire room went dark.

~ TWENTY-THREE ~

THE LIGHT WAS thickening, giving shape again to the morning when Alex made the turn off Edgecliff into the driveway of the old Cunningham place. His eyes were burning; his body protested the lack of sleep. He was exhausted

Alex unfastened his seat belt and leaned forward, onto the dashboard, to get a better look. He didn't see Sarah's car.

Drips of melting snow had frozen, in rows, along the steep gutters of the portico, pointing to the front door below.

He approached the front steps, nervously rehearsing what he would say to her when she opened the door. He reached his hand to grasp the doorknocker, but his eyes shifted downward.

There was a large brown envelope wedged inside the storm door. Alex opened the door and took the envelope. He read the writing on the front of the envelope, aloud.

Mary - signed contract inside. On my way home - making arrangements to have my grandmother moved closer to me within the next few days - Nothing here for me anymore. Please do your best to sell house ASAP.

Thanks, Sarah.

PS - You can reach me with the new number I gave you today. I finally got rid of that old phone for good. Thanks for everything -
Sarah. "

He was disheartened. Alex swallowed the lump in his throat. He looked upward and closed his eyes. Mumbling, he placed the envelope back in the door, closed it tightly and started back down the driveway to his car.

Alex hastily fell into the driver's seat and started the engine, but as he attempted to shift the car into reverse, he noticed that the position of the seat was farther back from where it should have been - not where he had left it. And when he attempted to shift the car from park to reverse, he was met with resistance. His jaw dropped open in shock.

Alex had meticulously maintained the car for years, never experiencing problems of any kind. But the gearshift had somehow become stuck and refused to move out of park.

He sat up straight and punched the steering wheel, in frustration. He turned off the engine and stepped back out of the car. The wind picked up; dozens of little stray tree branches tumbled across his path as he walked around the car.

Alex angrily leaned against the door of the old Mustang, took out his cell phone and began to make a call.

Just his luck! - *No* reception!

Alex paced up and down the driveway, desperately trying to find the magic spot that would allow him to call somebody for help. He could not believe that he couldn't get a call out, regardless of where he was in the driveway.

He headed down the street, continuing to search for cell reception. He reached the park entrance at the end of the street. Still no luck.

Had he driven into some alternative universe?

"The most *comprehensive* plan you offer and *this* is what I get?"

He flung the phone into a shallow snowdrift. With sheer exasperation in his voice, Alex shouted,

"Fuck!"

He regained his composure and bent over to retrieve his phone. He walked back up the walkway to the front step of the house again. Sinking down on the steps, he leaned against the railing, filled with a combination of anger and sadness.

Alex closed his eyes and rubbed them, trying to chase the headache away. He couldn't stop thinking about yesterday when he left Sarah. He put his head in his hands.

He was exhausted. It began to snow again, big wet flakes that wouldn't last very long - just enough to be an annoyance for Alex.

A little robin landed in the snow, beside the front step and began chirping loudly. Alex brought his face out from his hands just long enough to see it was just a bird, and buried his face again. The bird continued singing. Alex jumped up and glared down at the robin.

"What do *you* want?"

The bird stopped singing.

Alex chuckled, amused that he was able to interrupt the song. It made him feel in control - something he hadn't felt for some time. He sat back down on the step. The robin cocked its head and took a couple hops into the fresh snow.

"*What*?" He glared at the robin again.

The robin silently stared back at Alex. He shook his head and stood.

"I can't *believe* I am actually talking to a bird." Alex plunged his cold hands in his jacket pockets.

To his surprise, neither pocket was empty. From one, he pulled out a small piece of folded paper. Alex never kept things in his pockets - he was much too organized for that. This intrigued him. He carefully unfolded the paper.

A warm smile fell across his face as he recalled his conversation with his 4 year-old niece, Gracie, a few weeks before. On the paper were three sets of bird tracks, drawn in purple crayon. Gracie had signed it with her name in a heart and she had printed the title, *Stars*, at the top.

Alex refolded the paper, for safe-keeping, and reached back in the pocket to return it. But he quickly realized he was in the wrong pocket. There was something else in this one. He pulled out the keys he thought he had returned to Sarah last night. His heart raced.

The robin began chirping again.

Alex turned quickly, squinting into the rising sun. "*Look*!! ... I ..."

The words flung themselves back into his throat as he looked down at the tracks the little robin had left in the snow. His mouth dropped open.

Stars.

"*Stars*?" Then, as everything fell into place, in a much louder voice, he shouted, "*STARS!* "

Alex pulled the paper back out of his pocket and unfolded it. He shook it out, comparing it with the snow in front of him.

Alex walked quickly to his car, forgetting that there had been problems a few minutes earlier. Exhilarated, he jumped in, hit the ignition, and it fired up, without any reluctance at all.

He never hesitated as he backed out of the driveway.

~ TWENTY-FOUR ~

THE ELEVATOR DOORS PARTED. Sarah wearily walked out into the hallway, dragging her suitcase behind. She approached her apartment, where she was met by her neighbor and best friend, Jess, who was coming the other way.

Jess grabbed her by the arm, walking the rest of the way with her. "Honey, am I *glad* to see you! I was beginning to think you weren't coming home. I was ready to call out the Calvary!" After releasing Sarah from an embrace, Jess went on. "And at work ...*well* ..." Jess hesitated, placing his hands comically on his hips.

"Let's face it; there's only one voice for *Princess Penelope* - of the Planet *Proton.*"

Sarah stopped at her door and turned. She interrupted him. "Jess - I'm meeting Brad tonight."

Jess took her key and unlocked her door. "Here, let me get this for you." He rolled Sarah's suitcase into the apartment for her. She followed him, and threw her coat on the chair. Jess picked it up and hung it in the closet.

Sarah kicked off her shoes and sank into the couch, staring off in the distance. Sarah was silent. Jess lined her shoes up along the edge of the couch.

He sat next to her, massaging the back of her neck. "Honey - your neck muscles are tighter than Willie Nelson's headband. When are you going to learn to *relax*?"

Sarah quickly sat up and faced him. "Jess - you're my best friend. What do you think I should do?"

Jess took Sarah's hands in his and he looked her in the eyes. "It doesn't matter what I think, does it?" He put his arm around her shoulders. She leaned on him. "Just be happy, sweetie. Be *happy*."

Sarah smiled, but there was a lone tear rolling down her cheek.

~ TWENTY-FIVE ~

ALEX, SLEEP-DEPRIVED AND in dire need of a shave, staggered into the station, disheveled from driving all night.

He was spotted from across the room by Danny. A young rookie firefighter, Danny hadn't lost that *new job* sense of wonder yet, and was always the first to jump, head-first, into a conversation.

He poured coffee into a mug and walked it over to Alex. "You look like shit. You could use a cup of coffee."

Alex took the cup. There was no expression on his face.

"Where the hell have you been? You look like you've been up all night." He glanced at the computer monitor and continued. "Frank's out. They're on a call ... nothing big; some kids lit up some cans in the park - it was out by the time they got there. He should be back any minute. Sit down."

Alex felt a wave of exhaustion. He rested against the wall and took a big sip of the coffee. He studied the station house and before long, he had zoned out, deep in thought. The sputtering radio dispatches entangled themselves with the audio from the TV.

After backing into the station, the pumper shut off. The side door to the jump seat compartment opened and Frank stepped off the engine.

Danny informed Frank that Alex was there to see him. Frank showed concern as he walked into the common area, where he joined Alex.

Alex knew that it would take some time to explain to his brother that:

1. He didn't make it to Florida,
2. He'd found someone who set his heart on fire, and
3. He had a plan that may or may not involve breaking the law.

So he didn't. He just stood there, like an idiot.

Frank studied Alex's face for a moment, then he asked, "So, why aren't you half way to Florida?"

Alex stared straight back at Frank. "How much do you know about electrical wiring?"

Frank looked puzzled. "A little - but not enough to take on any kind of major project. I can get you the name of a good electrician who can ..."

Alex quickly interrupted him with, "No! *No electricians.* **Nobody** can know about this."

Frank was alarmed. He pulled Alex over to the side, out of earshot. Then, in a hushed tone, he probed, "Are you in some kind of trouble?"

They stepped outside onto the driveway. By his spirited hand gestures and facial expressions, it was obvious that Frank could not believe what Alex was telling him.

Frank was becoming increasingly more worried about his usually guarded, over-cautious little brother. He guided Alex back into the station and turned to face him.

He put his hand out and warned him. "Look - don't do anything yet. I'll tell Nick I have an emergency and I'll go over there with you."

He backed away, pointing a finger at Alex. "Wait *right here* for me." Frank took another step, then he quickly pivoted back around to face Alex and sternly said. "I mean it!"

Frank walked into the office and closed the door. Obviously preoccupied, he stared out at Alex, while fabricating a story, explaining to the chief that he needed to leave.

Nick had been with the company since his mid- twenties. He was now in his fifties - and he was the chief.

Alex paced nervously, back and forth in the hallway, outside the office, finally settling in one place, leaning, with his back against the wall. He turned his head, closed his eyes, rubbed them and opened them again.

He found himself looking at a wall that had been turned into a photo gallery. He wandered over to look at the pictures. Starting at the left, Alex walked by each picture, wondering what their stories were.

He observed portraits of young and old firefighters from the past and present time. He continued along and stalled at the middle of the gallery.

A photograph in the center was drawing him closer.

The picture was of a fireman; a captain, in his mid-sixties, in full dress uniform. Alex moved closer.

Another firefighter, Ryan, a captain in his mid-forties, walked past Alex and, noticing that he was studying the picture, stopped next to him. He smiled at the photograph. "Now there's a *true* legend."

Alex looked at him, then back at the picture.

Ryan elaborated a little. "You're looking at Chief Winston Cunningham; or *Wink*, as he liked to be called." He dusted the glass with a kerchief from his pocket. He took a deep breath before speaking again.

"He inspired us all to want to be better. Wink was good under pressure, and he knew instinctively how to handle tough situations."

Ryan pointed to another frame, just to the right of the portrait. It was a 1956 newspaper article about a local heroic firefighter. "That one was before my time, but it was how he lived his whole life. Wink was a hero in every sense of the word."

"On more than one occasion, I saw him jump off the truck in freezing temperatures, when it was still rolling to a stop because there were kids in a burning building; without even having his coat on yet."

Ryan's expression brightened as he recalled a particularly good memory. "Wink and Irene - that's his wife - they held this huge Christmas party at their house on the lake, every Christmas Eve from the year he joined the department, for as long as he lived."

The corners of his mouth turned upward as he went on. "They opened their house all night for everybody on city safety forces; on and off duty; even if it was only to stop by, grab a plate and take it with them. Wink would grill out in the back yard, even in the snow, and Irene baked for days getting ready for the party." He chuckled.

"Wink made the *best* homemade chili in the universe, and Christmas Eve was the *only* time he made it. His own secret recipe ...

he called it his *5-Alarm Firehouse Chili*." Ryan glanced over at the office again and lowered his voice.

"Nick's the only one who was ever able to get the recipe from him. And he guards it with his life. They couldn't do enough for us … never asked for anything in return. Christmas Eve was Wink and Irene's night." Ryan's face lit up with his next words.

"It was the one night of the year the whole city seemed to come together."

Alex picked up on the location of their house and Irene's name. "Did you say their house was on the lake?"

Ryan replied, "The old Cunningham place was on Edgecliff Drive, and had the best view in Cleveland of the skyline. It's still there, but we just heard that Irene isn't well and being moved into a facility out of state."

The pieces of the puzzle began to fall together for Alex. His eyes widened as Ryan continued.

"Every one of us, who was on the squad the night Wink died, remembers it like it was yesterday". Ryan turned Alex away from the office door and lowered the volume of his voice.

"I was driving ... when we pulled up to the apartments."
We were the first ones there, but it was already a really bad one. They told us everybody was out of the building. As we tried to assess the situation, I saw Nick." He motioned to the captain in the office, with Frank.

"He ran off, toward the back door of the building; I couldn't see if he had his radio or not. It was weird, because he never did anything like that before."

"We tried to call him to come back, but he didn't answer; he didn't even hesitate. Then we saw his radio lying on the ground next to the truck."

Ryan continued to tell the story, and shifted the recollection to present tense:

"We've got two companies standing there, three hoses going full throttle, but it just didn't seem like it was enough. We knew it was bad

when we started hearing and seeing the flames blowing the windows out."

"Then, this lady comes up to us, screaming that there are kids still in the building." Ryan sat down in a chair. Alex sat in another chair, across from him, giving his undivided attention to the story.

"I suit up, grab my gear and Nick's radio and head toward the back door, too. But, before I get to the door, I am yanked by the back of my coat, and thrown to the ground, and dragged back."

"I'm seeing stars, but I look up and who do I see, but "Wink Cunningham," standing over me." Ryan tensed slightly.

"It wasn't 15 seconds before the whole back half of the building explodes."

"Then Wink grabs my mask and tank and runs around to the front of the place. Then he disappears!"

"So I run back to the trucks, crazy because I don't know what the hell is going on. I was the only one who saw Wink; nobody can reach anybody over the radio; all we can do is keep the hoses on the fire."

"I never heard so much commotion in my life, even to this day."

Ryan's face reflected a note of preoccupation. Alex was no longer tired as he found himself riveted to Ryan's story.

"The wind picks up and, through the smoke, we only get glimpses of the building off and on for about 15 minutes... the longest 15 minutes of my life."

"Then, we see Nick, carrying a little boy out, followed by Wink, with the girl; EMS grabs them and gets them the hell out of there."

"But then, Nick turns around and goes back in; we thought he was nuts! Wink looks at the door and starts to follow behind Nick."

"We're yelling, "No! Come back", but neither one paid a bit of attention to us." Ryan rubbed his chin.

"So, I suit back up to go in. But before I get to the door, I am thrown back by another blast. The last thing I remember seeing was Nick's boots heading up the steps to the front door. Ryan showed Alex a scar on his temple.

"I think about that every time I look in the mirror."
Alex winced.

"So, we're all waiting for some kind of miracle; but nothing."
Ryan suddenly became quiet, choking up at the memory of the sight.

"I'm straining to see through the smoke, hoping and praying. Then, through the black, I see something coming out of the hole where the door used to be."

"It was Wink, and he was supporting Nick. He was barely conscious." He sat in a chair and clasped his hands nervously at the recollection.

"Within two minutes, the whole place collapses."

"They were okay?"

Ryan relaxed a little, but he spoke in q quieter tone. "Everybody was out. We all thought our prayers were answered."

"So, why did Nick go back in, if they already got the kids out?" Alex inquired.

Ryan inhaled deeply before answering the question. "Turns out that he had a feeling; he thought he felt something else when he found the 3 year-old boy under the bed. And, sure enough, he was carrying another 2 year-old boy when they came back out."

Alex was relieved. "But I thought you said that was the night Wink died."

"Wink was 68 years old. He'd been retired for three years. He just happened to be driving in the area when he realized there was a fire," Ryan explained. He glanced back at the portrait of Wink on the wall.

"Once a firefighter, always a firefighter. It gets into your blood, and stays with you for the rest of your life." Ryan looked down, sadly. "Wink got Nick and the boy over to the gurney and told Nick he did good."

"Then Wink looked right at me and told me it had to be an electrical fire. That was his special interest. He knew everything there was to know about electrical fires."

Ryan looked down and, just above a whisper, he said, "Then he collapsed. That was the last time anybody ever saw him alive."

"Heart attack?"

Ryan nodded.

Frank came out of the office and noticed they were looking at the picture on the wall. Ryan quickly added, as Nick followed Frank out of the office, "Nick doesn't talk about it … still blames himself. He thinks that if he hadn't gone back in the second time, Wink wouldn't have died that night."

As Frank approached them, he told Ryan, "I've got some stuff to take care of. I'll be back in a couple of hours." Frank walked toward the car with Alex.

After a few moments of conversation, Frank turned to Alex with a look of surprise. "Wait … you're telling me you were inside the old Cunningham place?"

~ TWENTY-SIX ~

ALEX AND FRANK WERE sitting at the table. Alex smiled as he showed Frank several images of Sarah on his phone, taken at his going-away party.

He picked up three different strings of old outdoor Christmas lights from the 1950's and showed them to his brother.

Frank was skeptical. "Are you bullshitting me? I can't believe these things *ever* worked, even when they were new. How many of these did you say there are?" Frank asked, examining one of the old light strings.

"A couple more than this." Alex replied.

Frank placed the string back down on the table. "How many is a *couple*?"

~ TWENTY-SEVEN ~

ALEX STOPPED AT THE door to the garage. Frank looked around, feeling a little suspicious. "We're not breaking and entering, are we? Because if that's what you've got in mind, I'm out of here."

Reaching in his pocket, Alex laughed and showed Frank the keys. "No, we're not breaking and entering. She gave these to me." He unlocked the door.

They entered the garage, pushing through boxes and years of accumulated stuff. Alex opened the door and led Frank up the stairs to the second-floor attic. They stopped at the top. Frank's mouth dropped open.

He stared at the stacks of boxes; too many to count; of old, 1950's outdoor Christmas lights and decorations, covered in more than 20 years of dust and dirt.

Frank opened one of the boxes and pulled out a tangle of three strings. He tried to untangle them. But he gave up, placing them back in the box. He shook his head. "This can't work, Alex. These haven't been used in over 20 years." He looked away and then back at Alex. "Plus, they are more than 30 years older than that! There's no way… that's just crazy."

He quickly started back down the stairwell to the ground floor, as if he was trying to escape something. He hurried, nervously, back to the car.

"Look, I'm not expecting you to take any of this on; just support me a little," Alex huffed, as he followed him.

Alex drove Frank back to the station, in silence. As they pulled up to the building, Alex put the car in park. He turned to Frank.

"You're not just my brother; you're my best friend. I just needed to tell you what I'm doing." Alex took a deep breath. "If you can help, that's great, but it's not a requirement."

Frank got out of the car and walked over to Alex's open window. He leaned in and just over a whisper, told him, "Alright, I won't say anything to anybody. Just be smart; and *think* before you do anything."

Alex nodded and smiled.

Frank reached in and gave Alex a hug. "I'll try to get over there tomorrow and see how it's going."

Worry etching his face, he stared and watched Alex drive away.

~ TWENTY-EIGHT ~

SARAH WAS ASLEEP ON her couch, covered by the throw that was usually over the back of the couch. She began to stir, waking from a six-hour sleep.

Her hair was a wreck. Feeling a little like Rip Van Winkle, she was disoriented at first, unsure of where she was, but slowly realized she was back home, in her own apartment.

Sarah was drawn by the smell of freshly brewed coffee. She staggered into the kitchen. The clock on the counter read 2:00 pm. She laughed and poured herself a cup of coffee.

"Oh, Jess - you take such good care of me."

She walked back to the living room and sunk into a chair. There was a knock at the door. Assuming it was Jess, Sarah opened it, without giving it any thought.

But instead of Jess, she was met by a delivery boy with an armful of red roses. He handed Sarah the roses. "I have a delivery for you, ma'am."

Sarah took the flowers and tipped the delivery boy. Sarah closed the door.

She read the card out loud, to herself. "Can't wait to see you tonight - fondly, Brad."

Her smile faded. Repeating the last part of the card, she said, *"Fondly?* That's it?"

The sound of another knock interrupted Sarah's thoughts. She set the flowers on the table and returned to the door. This time she looked in the peep hole, then she opened it.

Jess and two of his friends waltzed into her apartment carrying bags and boxes. She smiled, but she was puzzled. He gently guided Sarah into her bathroom and handed her a set of towels and the bathrobe from the back of the door.

"Honey, we love you dearly; truly, we do - but you might need just a tad bit of help to accent your best features." He gave her a grin. "When we're finished, your Brad won't know what hit him."

Sarah stepped out of the bathroom and pulled Jess aside and whispered, "But Jess ... don't they do *cabaret* stage hair and makeup?"

Jess threw up his hands, and erupted in laughter. "Only by night. Sarah, you are looking at two of the best cosmetic geniuses on the east coast."

"Trust me. They have *quite* an impressive clientele." Then, gently pushing her back into the bathroom, he added, "Now, *shoo*! ... the sooner you do your part, the sooner we can begin to ... create ..."

Jess turned away and began opening bags on hangers, laying dresses out across her bed.

Before long, the silence was replaced by the sound of running water coming from behind the closed door.

~ TWENTY-NINE ~

SARAH STARED, DUMFOUNDED BY her own reflection in the mirror. Jess joined her at the mirror, standing behind her, obviously pleased with the results. He grinned. More than anything, he was happy for her.

The black dress was sensuously cut, of slightly metallic silkiness that draped itself against Sarah like liquid mercury, with a teasing slit exposing just enough thigh to make anybody pray for a gentle breeze. And just as Jess requested ... heels ... suggestive, yet without drawing attention away from the main attraction.

Sarah's makeup was just enough to point out the fact that she didn't need war paint - she was a natural beauty.

Jess sighed. "Honey, I don't know where you've been hiding those bedroom eyes all this time but, after tonight, I'm afraid the cat will be out of the bag."

He turned Sarah to face him. "My child - you are *drop-dead gorgeous.*"

She giggled. "Is this really me?"

Jess smiled and kissed Sarah softly on the forehead. "At the risk of sounding like *Glenda, the Good Witch of the North*, "Sweetie - I think you had the power all along. You just didn't know it."

The alarm on Sarah's clock sounded. She walked to the table and turned it off. She noticed her glasses on the table, next to the clock. She started to put the glasses on, then set them back on the table. "I think I'll try to manage without these, for tonight, anyway." Jess picked the glasses up and placed them in their case. He dropped it into her purse.

"Don't forget - you are just as beautiful with them as you are without them," he told her, handing Sarah the bag.

~ THIRTY ~

THE GARAGE WAS DARK. Alex opened the side door and pulled the chain to the single-bulb light, revealing the inside of the old building. He looked upward to the rafters and the attic.

He climbed the stairs to the second floor. He brought boxes and everything he could find that looked like it could be decorations or lights, down to the main floor. He sat down on the garage floor, beginning the huge task of untangling the strings.

The sun began to make an appearance on the horizon, the black sky brightening to gray.

Alex was beginning to feel defeated before the fight even began. He looked upward to the sky. "What the hell have I gotten myself into?"

There was a knock on the wood frame of the open door. Alex glanced up from the tangled mountain of lights and noticed the silhouette of an older man standing in the light of the doorway.

He peeked in. "Hello there."

Alex looked at him as he entered the garage. Wearing a bulky winter jacket, the man appeared to be in his 60's. He stopped in front of Alex and looked straight at him. "I was on my morning walk and saw the light." Looking around the garage at the tangled mess, he scratched his head. "Looks like you've got quite a job on your hands, son."

Alex looked up with a nervous laugh. "Yeah, I may have taken on a little more than I can handle." He tossed a string of lights into a pile. "I'm trying to recreate history."

The man leaned over Alex taking one of the light strings in his hand and studied it. He looked at the diagram on the tablet. After a moment, he man stooped next to him.

"Need some help?"

Alex glanced up at him. "Do you know anything about this stuff?"

"Lights? Or women?" The man winked at him.

With a look of surprise, Alex met his eyes with a blank expression.

The man smiled. "You just have that *look* about you, son. Who is she?"

Alex sighed, welcoming the opportunity to finally open up about Sarah - even if it *was* to a complete stranger. He leaned against the wall and inhaled deeply. "I think I might be too late."

He brushed the dirt off the knees of his jeans with his hands. "Oh, I *don't* know. We have *nothing* in common. Sarah is so creative; she sees everything through different eyes than me." He stared into empty space. "I don't have a creative bone in my body. I wouldn't even know where to start."

The man picked up the diagram on the tablet, looking around at the open boxes on the floor of the garage, and said, "Oh, I wouldn't be *too sure* about that. This looks like one of the most creative undertakings I've ever seen."

Alex tossed another string of lights, adding to the pile as he took a step to the right. He put his hands in his pockets to keep them warm.

"She told me I'm *predictable*."

The man raised an eyebrow slightly. "Is that *bad*?"

Alex began pacing back and forth in the garage, wringing his hands. "I don't know *anything* anymore! I used to be so *sure* of everything!"

Still sitting on the garage floor, among the lights, the man gave Alex a kind smile and questioned him. "So, what changed?"

Alex quickly spun back toward him. "This is **exactly** what I'm talking about!" Alex exclaimed, flapping his arms about in frustration. "*Look* at me! I'm telling my troubles to a guy I have *never seen* before!"

Then, regretting his impulsive rage, he apologized. "No offense. It's just *not* who I am!" He squatted next to the man and looked him in the eyes. "I am a *Communications* Specialist. It's my *job*! And I can't even find a way to *reach* Sarah."

He reached up and rubbed his forehead, leaving behind a smudge. "I have *all* the latest and greatest technological devices, and *what* does it get me?" Alex stood, restlessly and went on.

"She's *gone* and I have *no way* to tell her I want her to give me another chance. She has a new phone with a number I don't know." He outstretched his arms, waving them in frustration and he shouted, "How am I supposed to *communicate* if I have *no way* to communicate?"

Alex paused for a moment. His voice lowered in volume. "Oh - you couldn't *possibly* get what I'm talking about - how *could* you?"

The man looked serious for a moment. He got even closer to Alex and he stopped right in front of him. A smiling twinkle appeared in his eyes.

"The trouble with you young folks is that you give up too easily."

Alex was surprised and stepped back.

The man stepped closer, pointing a lecturing finger at him. "Just because I may be *past my prime* does not mean I can't *relate*." He took a deep breath and went on. "When I was a young man, we had *lots* of ways to communicate. We just had to put a little *more effort* into it."

Alex rolled his eyes and smiled. "You're not going to tell me about *smoke signals*, are you?

The man placed a heavy hand on Alex's shoulder. "The most important event in my *whole* life happened because I sent a telegram." He turned away from Alex, then back again.

"You **have** heard of the *telegram*, haven't you?

"Yeah, it was like an email; right?"

The man chuckled, moving along. "Something like that." He reached into a box. "As for getting your Sarah to come back; I'm sure you will think of something; you are far more creative than you think you are." He hesitated for a moment. He pulled on more light strings.

"Now, just *what is it* you're trying to accomplish here, son?"

Alex picked up the sketch Sarah's grandfather had drawn with the detail and location of all of the decorations and lights, and showed it to him. The man scrubbed his hands over his face before lowering them to grip his knees

The man grinned, as if he was trying to keep from laughing, and took the sketch from Alex. He turned the diagram upside down from the way Alex had it and handed it back to him. "Well, this is a start." A laugh bubbled up from his belly. "You're over-thinking it," he said.

He glanced across the yard, strode down the driveway and gave Alex a hard glance. "Come on son, we've got some work to do!" He winked again and began gathering strings, blowing and shaking off dirt and dust as he took them out the door.

Alex looked confused at first, but he scrambled to get up and followed the man onto the driveway.

~ THIRTY-ONE ~

ALEX WAS STANDING IN the driveway, staring back at the house. The man came out of the garage with two boxes under his arm. He approached Alex and set the boxes on the driveway, in front of him.

"We missed a couple; not sure what they are, but I know you'll find the perfect place for them." He grinned, and gazed back at the house.

"I think we did just fine, don't you, son?"

The sun was beginning to fade. The man flashed a big smile and slung an arm around Alex. They walked down the driveway together. He turned to the house and reminded Alex of what he needed to do.

"Now just switch everything on in the right order. Don't panic; don't *overanalyze*." He winked. "And remember, son - it takes all of the fun out of it if you have to have a reasonable explanation for everything."

Alex picked up the two boxes. Out of the corner of his eye, he caught the glint of late afternoon sunlight hitting the lake; a sure sign that time was running out if he was going to finish by nightfall.

Off in the distance, figures in the form of Frank, Ryan and Danny approached.

The man suddenly appeared to be uncomfortable – in a hurry. He fidgeted as he reached out to shake Alex's hand. "Listen, I've really got to run."

"You *are* going to stay here for this, *aren't* you?"

The corners of the man's eyes crinkled a little as he squinted into the setting sun, giving Alex a one-armed, genuine hug and pat on the back. "You will *never know how much* I would love to ... but I *really can't* stay. It was good to meet you, son." He paused and, seeing the disappointment in Alex's face, he inhaled and added, "If there's a way, I will try to stop back by to see the place."

Alex insisted, telling him, "Well, at *least* stay long enough so I can introduce you to my brother, Frank."

But when he turned back, the man was already gone.

~ THIRTY-TWO ~

BRAD WAS LEANING ON the bar, waiting for Sarah, flanked by the usual harem of women clamoring to be seen with him. His insincere smile could be spotted from across the room. Sarah draped her winter coat over her arm and took a deep breath.

The atmosphere changed noticeably as Sarah entered the room. Conversations halted in mid-stream as she walked past each table. Not only was Sarah gorgeous - she was exuding an air of self-confidence that nobody had ever seen or felt before that moment.

Sarah approached Brad at the bar. He had his back to her, but when he sensed something was happening behind him, he turned and was in awe of what Sarah had become.

Brad raised his glass to his lips, but he lost his grip on it, and had to quickly recover it before he dropped it completely. His slightly shaky hand hastily set the still-full glass down on the bar.

He made no attempt to hide his head-to-toe inspection. Everybody around him became invisible, as Brad fell *hopelessly* in love.

Sarah hugged Brad. He forcefully kissed her hard - almost in a hurry to make up for lost time. She dropped her coat on the floor. Taking her hands in his, he stepped back from her, surveying *his prize*.

"Sarah, you look fabulous! *How long* did this *take*?"

Perturbed by Brad's inquisition, Sarah answered him with her own question. "*How long* do you **think** it took??"

Brad grabbed Sarah and kissed her again, quickly pressing his body against hers. Sarah tightened. She felt cold inside.

"Sweetheart, what's wrong? You seem ... *different.*" he said, pulling back with a puzzled look.

Sarah was becoming increasingly more uncomfortable as the realization set in that maybe she did not have to *settle*. She pulled completely away from Brad's grip.

Glancing to the glass on the bar, next to Brad, she contemplated re-enacting a scene from an old Hollywood movie she had just watched a few days ago. The *old* Sarah wouldn't have considered doing anything like that.

Well, maybe it's time for the new Sarah to make an appearance.

Sarah picked up Brad's glass and tossed back the entire contents in one fell swoop. She stiffened and the color drained from her face.

Scotch! God, I HATE SCOTCH!

Then she smiled gently at him. "Brad - I'm not sure what has happened to me. But I *can* tell you that it's not about the way I *look* at all." She took a deep breath. "It goes much deeper than that. And maybe, in some small way, I should thank you."

Brad gripped her arm tightly, as if he was trying to keep her from escaping. "Sarah - what's *wrong* with you? Whatever it is - let's *talk* about it."

Sarah shook her head. "It's not you, Brad - it's about *me* this time. And I have to tell you - I would be lying if I said I'm not a little scared."

The light sparkled in her eyes as she went on. "But I am so excited at the same time! And, you know *what*?" She reached in her purse and pulled out her glasses, clumsily placing them crookedly on her nose, before snatching them off, replacing them back in their case. "I'm going to wear these whenever I need them."

She lightly touched his arm. "I honestly wish you everything good. I will never forget you, Brad."

Sarah picked her coat up off the floor and kissed Brad goodbye on the cheek. She slowly turned and walked out of the restaurant, leaving his jaw on the floor.

It was all a big blur for Sarah, but she held her head high, continuing through the restaurant and out the door.

~ THIRTY-THREE ~

OUTSIDE, ON THE STREET, Sarah held back her emotions for as long as she could. She stopped just out of the sight line of the bar window. The cocktail was beginning to affect *command central*, in her head. And her equilibrium.

A quiet sob rose and the tears began. From out of the shadow of the doorway a soft, kind voice addressed her.

"Hey, Princess ... If I had a white horse, could I convince you to ride off into the sunset with me?"

It was Jess.

He was leaning against the exterior brick wall of the restaurant. Strikingly handsome, his face was filled with empathy.

Sarah sniffed and forced a smile.

Damn. He looks like James Bond, leaning against that wall and all. So absurdly unfair.

"I thought you'd be at home, working on the new episode."

"I've been watching you from the window." Jess dabbed her eyes with his handkerchief.

Sarah hiccupped and let out a sad little giggle. "Just my luck. My very own stalker ... *dazzlingly* good-looking ... *and he's already taken.*"

Jess winked at her. "I had a feeling our little bird might find her wings tonight."

With his arm around her shoulders they began walking together. Jess continued. "To say I'm so proud of you would be an understatement."

Sarah sighed as she rested her head on his shoulder. "I'm beginning to think there's nobody out there for me." She stopped and faced him. "Jess, would you take me home?"

"Of course, princess," he said, giving her a hug. Jess smiled and raised his hand to hail a cab. The cab stopped and Jess opened the door for Sarah.

To the cab driver, Jess, in one of his signature cartoon voices, made a request: "To the planet *Proton*."

The driver gave him a *look*, indicating that he obviously knew nothing about kids' cartoons. Jess smiled and cheerfully added, "Okay - *Plan B* – "You can just drop us at the corner of York and First." Sarah settled in her seat.

The moment was interrupted by Sarah's phone. She fumbled and took the phone from her purse.

"Hi Mary. How's Colorado?" Jess tried not to eavesdrop, but he couldn't help wondering what Mary was saying on the opposite end of the conversation that was getting Sarah so wound up.

"But, Mary - the house isn't *really* on the market yet. How can you *already* have a potential buyer?" She smiled, and then frowned a little, appearing confused. "*Really*?" She made a face at her reflection in the cab window.

"But, Mary - I don't think the few little things I didn't finish up will make a difference."

Jess detected an increase in Sarah's blood pressure as she listened to Mary.

"That's the day after Christmas! You won't even be back in town until Christmas night. It only gives me a couple of days to get back and get everything ready for a showing. By *myself*! And I have to be in *New York* to get my grandmother settled in!" She paused.

"*Okay - stop hyperventilating*! I'll push back the moving date for my grandmother. I will head back in the morning and you can show it on the 26th!"

Jess looked at Sarah sideways and tilted his head, trying to hear what the fuss was all about. Sarah spoke again.

"Alright. I will meet with you early in the morning, and we can do the showing in the late afternoon." She smoothed out the wrinkles in her dress and ended the call.

"Have a nice Christmas with your family. Call me when you get back to Cleveland." She sighed and looked at Jess.

"I have to go back to Cleveland. I might have a buyer for the house."

Jess hugged her and smiled. "That's *wonderful*! He clasped his hands together. "Just think - you might get what you want for Christmas this year after all!"

Sarah settled back against him. Jess brushed the lingering tear from her cheek. And they headed home.

~ THIRTY-FOUR ~

FRANK, RYAN AND DANNY APPROACHED Alex. All three appeared stunned with what Alex had been able to do to the old Cunningham place.

Leaning in toward Alex, with concern, Frank told him, "I hope you know what you're doing." He looked around. "This could be *one colossal disaster*, you know." Then he softened and touched Alex on the shoulder.

"Look, Alex, we all think it's a great idea, but the reality is that you're taking a *big risk*; you could be *killed*, and the house ..." He glanced up and down the street.

"… maybe the *whole neighborhood* could go up in flames. This is *really* old stuff."

Ryan and Danny began wandering, taking a closer look at the massive quantity of lights, covering the old house. They were speechless.

"And, I could lose my job; we *all* could, if this gets out. We should be stopping you," Frank continued, leaning in closer to him.

But Alex was determined. There was no turning back. "I understand; you need to go. I'm not mad. I know how hard you've worked to get where you are; the best damn Lieutenant this department will ever know." His voice was beginning to show more emotion.

"The last thing I want is for you to lose your job. But I'm going through with this." He smiled at Frank and picked up the last box the man had brought out to him. He turned to walk away.

Danny shook his head. "I don't see how one person could have *physically* done all of this in one day."

Alex pulled on one flap of the last box. He stopped and looked at the trio. "I had help. It wasn't just *me*."

They looked surprised.

Alex elaborated. "One of the neighbors; the old guy from down the street, helped me do all of this." He added, "I wanted you to meet him, but he had somewhere to go. Maybe he'll be back around later."

Frank looked dumbfounded. Ryan looked at Frank, then to Danny. And together, they *all* looked back at Alex.

Frank confessed, a little sheepishly. "We talked to all the neighbors - we *had* to - to make sure we knew who else lives on the street ... you know ... in case you went through with this craziness."

Alex raised an eyebrow.

"But, we didn't tell anybody what you were doing."

Danny added, "There are only young families on this street. We got a head count from everyone in case of an emergency."

"Nobody said anything about an older man," Ryan told him.

Alex continued walking away from them toward the house. "Maybe I heard him wrong." He made a frustrated gesture with his hands." It doesn't matter; there's no way I could have done this without him." He faced them again.

"I'll see you later."

Frank, Ryan and Danny couldn't look at each other. Slowly, they began to leave the scene, one-by-one while Alex perched himself on the front step and began opening the last boxes, one at a time.

He immediately recognized the first one. He opened the flaps and lifted out the star that Sarah's grandfather had hung on the rooftop peak. He set it aside and moved on to the next box.

First, Alex pulled out crumpled paper. Under a string of old lights, he found a slightly smaller red box. He shook his head and chuckled.

… *The unveiling of the long lost treasures.*

He carefully lifted the top off the box. Alex dug through a variety of bracelets made out of ancient chewing gum wrappers and a couple of vintage birthday cards.

He turned the box upside down, shaking it so the rest of the contents fell out. There was still something wedged against the bottom of the box. He reached in and pulled out a large red envelope. Glitter fell from the old seams that had come apart over time. He carefully opened the envelope and removed the contents.

Alex was flabbergasted; he felt like he had stepped back in time, staring at the valentine he'd made for the girl on the playground, all those years ago.

But ... how...?

The alarm on his watch sounded. He glanced down. There was no time for guessing games. He quickly placed everything back in the box and headed for the garage. But just as he passed his car in the driveway, he stopped.

Another virtual light bulb.

Alex hopped into his car. He hastily started it, backed out of the driveway and onto the street.

~ THIRTY-FIVE ~

THE CEMETARY LOOKED THE SAME as it had twenty years ago at his parent's memorial service; the last time Alex had been there.

The ground was covered in a fluffy blanket of white. The sky was fading into the shadows of sunset as gauzy clouds flirted with the heavens.

As Alex approached the gravestones, he could tell they had been recently cleaned off. A bouquet of fresh flowers lay on the snow, in between them, dwarfing the two single red roses he had brought with him. There was no doubt in his mind the bouquet had been left there by Frank.

The only other time Alex had been there, he had been racked with guilt.

Through the years, he had come to accept that his parents were really gone. But the guilt and the blame he had placed on himself for not showing them how much he loved them had deepened. He had struggled ever since.

For years, he had fielded questions about his mom and dad from his friends and colleagues. Like tiny darts, everybody constantly threw questions at him.

But the one person he really needed to talk about his feelings with was the one person he hadn't been able to reach.

Himself.

And from that fateful day on; the afternoon of the funeral; Alex had completely shut himself out.

Alex knelt down and laid a rose on each of the graves. He inhaled deeply. "Mom ... Dad ... I'm sorry. I should have come back a long time ago."

He could picture them there with him; a vision from so many years ago; his mother with her arms out, waiting for one of those hugs he avoided, and his father with his hands perched firmly on his hips, sporting that funny grin. It gave him comfort. He smiled.

Alex sat back in the snow, scooting his butt until he rested in front of his parents' graves. He dusted the snow off the knees of his jeans.

Feelings Alex didn't normally allow surged up inside him. It had been so much easier to always be in control. His heart stuttered. "I'm sorry I was such a bad son. And I'm so sorry I was afraid to show you how much I loved you. But I did." His voice cracked.

"I still do."

Getting comfortable in the moment, Alex became more relaxed and laid on his back in the snow between the graves. He stared up at the darkening sky, his hands folded on his chest, reminiscent of a patient on the couch at a session with a Psychiatrist.

"After you died, I pretty much lost myself. I refused to let anybody in. Especially Frank." He inhaled, and then he blew out, in relief. "I know now that was wrong."

"*God*, Mom ... you have no idea what Frank did for me. He gave up so much for that *screwed-up, defiant, asshole* 12-year-old kid."

Alex looked upward. His mouth went flat. "Sorry ... I know how much you *hate* swearing." He finished explaining. "But I really gave him a run for his money. He should have sent me off to a foster home after what I put him through."

"So much has happened since we talked." Alex breathed in a deep breath, blew it out and smiled. "*... A whole lifetime ...*"

He laughed softly. "*Dad* ... wait till you hear this!" He hesitated as if he was waiting for a reply from his father.

"You know that dilapidated old brewery building on Franklin; the one that you always told us they used to shoot the 4th of July fireworks off from, *back in the day*, when you were a kid?"

Alex paused. Then he waved his hands in the air, letting out a laugh that echoed throughout the cemetery. "They just had their grand opening. It's a *micro-brewery*!" He quickly re-folded his hands across his chest.

"Crap. Sorry, Dad. I don't know if you even know what a *micro-brewery* is." Alex paused, and then grinned, as if he was responding to a *communique from beyond.*

"*I know.* **"Use the words in context to help define the phrase."**

His father had been a highly regarded high school literature teacher, which had been partially responsible for their failure to communicate effectively during those final months.

"How can I begin to tell you about what's happened in my life over the last month?" His forehead wrinkled. "Mom, you would love Sarah. She's a lot like you. She's got a wild imagination - nothing like me. You were right when you told me I didn't inherit the *fun* gene."

"And Dad, I know Sarah would *love* hearing all your cornball jokes - even the ones that weren't that funny. She has this laugh ... so contagious that your cheeks would burn from laughing with her."

The wind off the lake picked up, enveloping him in a warm breeze. The hair on his arms stood up. It was almost as if he was being asked a question. His voice broke on that. He felt a sudden rush of loss - of grief.

Normally, Alex made it a point to keep his emotions deeply buried. Tonight he deliberately pulled them out and made himself face them.

"Yes," Alex said as he finally let his tears fall for his parents - and his life. "Believe me - I fought it with *everything* I had in me. But yes - I think I love her."

And over the course of the next twenty minutes, Alex filled his mom and dad in on the last twenty years of his life story and the most recent chapter with Sarah.

~ ~ ~ ~ ~

In the distance, lights were beginning to come on along the shoreline, illuminating the bluish-lavender sky, indicating that time was running out.

Alex stood up from his gut-spilling reunion with his parents, and swiveled back for a last look, as he walked away.

He did a double-take.

Left behind in the spot where he had just spent the last twenty minutes was an imprint in the snow. Alex shook his head in an attempt to clear the thought.

But it sure looked like an angel to him.

Crazy ... I think I made a snow angel. He laughed to himself as he walked back to his car.

In his haste, Alex had neglected to notice something else about that particular snow angel.

There were no footprints leading away from it.

~ THIRTY-SIX ~

DANNY, RYAN AND FRANK walked into the firehouse. Their faces were expressionless. No audible conversation between them could be heard, but the tension could have been cut with a knife.

The building was filled with the most enticing aroma of *Wink's 5-Alarm Firehouse Chili,* which had become a holiday tradition, and had earned the distinct reputation of single-handedly making it worth having to work the holiday shift.

An on-duty Lieutenant peeked out the office window, then yelled at them.

"Hey! Aren't you guys supposed to be off duty all night? It's *Christmas Eve*! Do you *know* how many of us would give anything to trade places with you? What are you *doing*? *Go home*!!"

They sat in the common area, saying nothing, deep in thought. Feeling guilty, they began conversing with each other. The exchange was intense.

Everything went silent again. Another on-duty firefighter walked in, drinking a cup of coffee and leaned on the wall next to the framed photograph of Wink.

Legend has it that firefighters have an unspoken language, known only to each other. This was the perfect example of that.

All three felt a simultaneous tingling rush as the hair on the back of their necks stood on end. They each stared at the picture as if it was a sign and, one-by-one; they stood and put their jackets back on, without even looking at each other.

They scrambled to leave, but they found themselves piled up at the doorway, *3 Stooges-Style*, as they were stopped by the intimidating, six foot, six inch figure of the no-nonsense-chief, Nick, at the door, blocking the way out.

Meeting them, coming from the galley, Nick wiped his greasy, chili-covered hands across the bib of his apron. To suggest he was suspicious and pissed would have been a major understatement.

"Alright!" His booming voice bounced back and forth between them. "This is *bullshit*! You guys are up to something - you've been acting funny ever since you walked in here." Then he stared straight at Frank.

"Now, which one of you is going to tell me what the *hell* is going on?"

They all went limp and plunked back down, with the knowledge that they would have to tell the chief where they had been. In the silence that followed, they all looked at each other. The visible deflation in their faces was painful. They knew they could never get back to the house in time.

It was over.

~ THIRTY-SEVEN ~

ALEX ENTERED THROUGH THE main doors and approached the desk at the nurse's station. The melodic sounds of Christmas carols wafted throughout the home.

Father McBurney, along with a dozen from his flock, was spending Christmas Eve with the residents.

Alex held the glass door open for the father, whose arms were loaded with bags of ice and a punch bowl. Alex reached out and caught a bag of ice from him, just as it slipped from his grip. He nodded and grinned at Alex.

"Thanks ... so much for *divine intervention*." Regaining control over the remaining bag, he added, "Hey, be sure and stop by the nurse's station for a cup of my punch."

A nurse chuckled as the two men approached the desk.

"There's nothing like *Father McBurney's Famous Holiday Punch*. Once you've had it, it will ruin you for any other punch."

Father McBurney set the punch bowl on the counter. "I'll be right back with the rest of it." He turned and headed back to the parking lot.

There was something about Father McBurney; something that made him stand apart from the other men of the cloth that graced the halls of the facility.

Maybe it was the *Rock and Roll* T-shirts he thought he cleverly concealed under his jackets. Or maybe it was his smirk when he knew you weren't telling the entire truth.

Whatever it was, Father McBurney had earned a special place in the hearts of the residents and staff at the home. In their eyes, he was the true equivalent of a rock star.

In her late fifties, the nurse reminded Alex of a pudgy, jolly little elf. She stood. Recognizing him from his previous visits to see Irene, was surprised that she found him even more handsome than before. She decided right there and then that she liked the rough, slightly rugged, unshaven look.

Alex nonchalantly made an attempt to hide his nervousness as he approached the desk. "How's Irene today?"

The nurse tilted her head to one side. "Irene had a rough night. Very restless. She didn't sleep much. We had to give her a sedative. She's a little upset at the thought of moving away." She glanced back at Irene's door, then to Alex again, and whispered,

"Just between you and me … I'm not so sure this move is the best thing for her right now."

Alex leaned in closer to the nurse, and spoke in a hushed tone, taking full advantage of her obvious infatuation with him. "Can I ask you something? … I mean *completely off the record*?" He guided her away from the desk, out of earshot range of the others.

Then Alex really turned on the charm. In a smooth-talking manner, he said, "You know, I was thinking … Wouldn't it be nice if Irene could spend *one last* Christmas at home …especially since she's being moved away?"

With a look of bafflement, the nurse looked back at him. "What do you mean?"

Alex touched her elbow, then traced her upper arm slightly and, taking note of the name on her badge, whispered softly, "Rose, do you think there's any way I could take Irene back home tonight? It's Christmas Eve ..."

Rose looked inquisitively at Alex. She slowly shook her head. "Oh, I don't think I can let you take her out of here." She reached over and opened a file folder. After flipping through a page or two, she asked Alex, "Her granddaughter is in New York, isn't she? Does she know about this?"

Alex didn't answer. He quickly avoided her question. Meeting her eyes, Alex gave her his best *puppy-dog* look, usually reserved for women he knew were lusting after him.

Father McBurney surfaced again, pushing a man wearing a Santa hat, in a wheelchair, approaching the nurse's station from the west hall. Rose smiled over at them. Alex held his breath and faced the opposite direction, desperately trying to fly under the radar.

Don't stop. Don't ask me anything.

Alex wasn't particularly religious, but he knew it would be impossible to lie to a priest.

They continued down the hall. Alex exhaled.

Rose hesitated for a moment, in thought. She sighed. She couldn't resist Alex. It was like he was a big magnet and she was a bag filled with metal shavings.

They leaned together for the next few minutes, collaborating and developing a conceivable plan.

~ THIRTY-EIGHT ~

LIGHTS OFF, ALEX PULLED the Mustang up to the delivery entrance. Leaving the engine running, he quickly jumped out, ran around to the passenger side and opened the door. Rose helped Alex get the unsteady Irene safely into the car.

Irene smiled appreciatively back at Rose. After Irene was securely inside, Rose tucked her scarf into her coat and slammed the door shut. With a full heart, she blew Irene a kiss.

Alex walked toward the drivers' side but he stopped as he watched Rose reach for the door to the building. He called out,

"Rose! *Wait* a minute!" She paused. He hurried back over to the delivery door and caught up with her.

No sooner had she turned around when Alex enveloped her in a big bear hug. He planted a sweet kiss on her cheek.

Snow began to fall in tiny, delicate flakes. He touched her cheek and smiled. "Merry Christmas, Rose." He winked at her. "And thank you."

Rose was very moved by his gesture. She caressed the spot on her cheek where Alex had kissed her; a little dazed.

Quickly regaining her senses, she gently shoved Alex back toward the car. "*Hurry*! You don't have much time before somebody realizes she is missing. And ..." she shouted as he opened the car door, "*Merry Christmas!*"

Taillights disappeared into the early evening sky as Rose locked the door to the delivery entrance. She glanced around to make sure she hadn't been seen, and tucked the keys safely into her pocket.

~ THIRTY-NINE ~

FEELING MORE THAN a little suspicious, Rose carefully perused the lobby. She hastily headed back to the nurses station, running against time.

Picking up speed, she flew down the hall, on her way back to the desk. She rounded a corner. And she stopped *dead* in her tracks.

Meeting her, coming from the opposite direction, was none other than Father McBurney, balancing two Styrofoam cups, filled with his famous punch, in his hands. He was so startled that he instinctively raised one of his hands to shield his face, forcing the contents of the cup to spray over his face.

And up his nose.

The man of the cloth blew out a quiet breath and stared straight in Rose's eyes. She looked very guilty, like the *cat that ate the canary*, even though she tried desperately to hide it.

She reached to wipe the punch off Father McBurney's face. "Oh, Father - I am *so sorry*! I should have been watching where I was going."

Father McBurney reached in his pants pocket for his handkerchief and finished mopping his face. Slightly annoyed, he asked, "And *wherever on earth was it* that you were going to in such a hurry?" His stern expression suddenly morphed into a forgiving smile. In a kinder, gentler voice, he asked her, "Rose - *What is it*? *What* has got you so jittery?"

Rose couldn't answer him. She couldn't even bring herself to look at him. Father McBurney placed his handkerchief back in his pocket. He sensed Rose's uneasiness. He touched her arm.

"Rose - What is troubling you so?"

She hesitated. Then she looked deep into Father McBurney's eyes, searching for forgiveness. "Father, *forgive* me. I have a confession to make."

Father McBurney was quietly surprised. "Rose, I didn't know you were Catholic."

"I'm not."

Father McBurney escorted Rose down the hall, as she filled him in on what had transpired with Irene and Alex.

A full range of expressions on Father McBurney's face indicated shock and dismay as Rose described, in detail, how she was an accomplice in Irene's kidnapping.

As Rose concluded her story, Father McBurney slowly shook his head and gave her a kind, understanding look of disapproval. "Oh, Rose. *What a tangled web we weave, when first we practice to deceive.*"

Another nurse appeared from around the corner. In a mild panic, she ran to them. "Have you seen *Irene*? She wasn't at dinner. And she's not in her room!"

Father McBurney and Rose looked at each other.

Rose knew what she had to do. She inhaled deeply and began spilling out her confession.

"I ..."

But before Rose had a chance to complete what she was going to say, Father McBurney clutched her arm, stopping her from finishing her sentence. He looked intently past the nurse, and hastily downed the entire contents of the remaining, unspilled cup.

He quickly glanced upward, as if to ask for forgiveness, then he blurted out, "... I think I saw her, just a *few minutes* ago ... in the activity room."

"The **activity room**? *Why* would she be in the activity room?"

Father McBurney motioned down the hallway as he began a slow trot to assist in the search for the missing Irene. He gestured to Rose as he passed her.

Rose was taken aback. She had no idea Father could be so good with a bluff.

"I'll go *this* way and look for her." He caught her eye. "*Rose!* - go with her and help her search *every inch* of the activity room." He gave her a wink. "You *know* how Irene likes to play Hide and Seek."

The other nurse hesitated, in a daze for a moment, but she followed Rose, muttering, "*Hide and Seek?*"

As the pursuit for Irene continued, Father McBurney crafted multiple creative roadblocks, in a desperate attempt to stall for time before the realization of what had actually happened set in.

The hunt that followed was wacky, yet heartwarming as Father McBurney quickly transformed himself into a master of deception, leading the troop on a zig-zagging *Wild Goose Chase*, up and down the hallways of the home.

~ FORTY ~

ALEX PULLED INTO THE driveway and helped Irene out of the car. She gazed up, marveling at the decorations on the house, although nothing was lit up yet.

She inhaled deeply. "Oh *Alex*, did *you* do all this?" Her eyes scanned the very top peak.

Alex smiled. His eyes followed her, moving upward to the roof of the house.

*The star. Crap. You forgot **the star!***

Alex realized that there was no star on the top peak of the roof. He rushed to get Irene inside, out of the cold.

"Let's get you inside, where it's warm."

Alex got Irene into the house and onto the living room sofa. He made her comfortable with pillows and blankets. And he turned on the Christmas tree lights.

He sat by Irene and smiled. "Can I get you anything before I go back out?"

Irene patted his hand. "Oh, sweetheart, you have already done more than you know. You have given one crazy, old lady the best Christmas gift *ever!*" She smiled. "You go on. I'll be just fine, Alex."

But as he walked toward the door, Irene called him back. "You know, there is one thing ..." Alex returned to her side. "Would you turn on the television for me?"

It was an older TV, with no remote control but, eventually, he managed to power it on. He backed away as the image and sound track became clearer.

Irene clasped her hands together, giggling. Alex imagined what she must have looked like as a little girl.

"Oh, this is one of my favorite movies of *all time*! Wink and I watched this old *John Wayne* movie every opportunity we had. We used to laugh and laugh and *laugh*!"

Alex became immersed in a mud-slinging fight scene playing out on the TV screen as the straight-shooting rancher drove his point home.

"You know, I haven't lost my temper in 40 years. But Pilgrim ... you could have really hurt somebody!"
"Somebody 'oughta belt you with this thing."
"But I won't ... I won't."
"... The HELL I won't!"

Alex chuckled, and then full out laughed, as he watched the characters in the legendary movie, *McLintock!,* slide down the hill into the mud. He realized that he hadn't laughed like that in years. He glanced over at Irene. "I'll be back for you when it's time."

But Irene didn't even hear him, she was so absorbed in the movie. Alex slipped out the front door as the sound track followed him.

~ FORTY-ONE ~

THE POSSE HAD INCREASED in numbers as the hunt for Irene continued into its second hour.

The head nurse flagged down Father McBurney, in the south hall. "I think we need to call the police!"

Father McBurney quickly bolted in the opposite direction, out of breath, feverishly waving his arms and shouting, "Maybe she went *this* way!" He pointed to a utility closet. "How about *this* door? *Come on!*"

All gears shifted and everybody followed the father.

The head nurse reached for the doorknob. She grabbed it and stopped suddenly. It was locked.

She raised her voice in frustration. "*Who* locked this door? It's *never* locked!"

Father McBurney turned and pointed back in the direction they had just come from. "Who has the *key*?" Everybody stared at each other in silence. He paused and hollered, "Well then, let's *go find the key!*"

The entourage scurried down the east hall, following him blindly, like lemmings to an unknown fate. It was chaotic - and it was madcap.

As the crowd faded out of sight and voices became more distant, an outline appeared from the shadows.

The indistinguishable figure reached out and placed a small key in the lock. The hand turned the key slowly and the door opened. Pulled back a little, the door was left cracked, slightly ajar.

Rabbi Goodman smiled as he backed away from the closet. Suspiciously glancing around, to make sure he hadn't been detected, he proudly rushed back down the hallway, out of sight, and rejoined the search party.

~ FORTY-TWO ~

ALEX WAS CARRYING THE broken star. He walked slowly out into the yard. He hesitated for only a moment before he climbed the ladder to the first roof. As he scaled the steep incline to the second level, he became aware of the sharp increase in his heartbeat. He took a deep breath and he hoisted himself onto the lowest point of the third level, ascending the peak of the steep rooftop.

There were three charred pieces that were barely hanging onto the star - a result of when Sarah had shorted it out. Alex reached in his pocket and pulled out the almost empty roll of electrical tape he had been using on the lights that afternoon. He reinforced the loose fragments but it still looked pathetic.

Looking down at the weary star in his hand, he whispered, "I know you can't light anymore. But, just between you and me, you still belong as high up as I can get you."

Alex hung the sad star on a rusty nail. He tucked the cord behind it, to hide the fact that it was supposed to light up. He stood, almost losing his balance, but he caught himself.

And he smiled.

Alex worked his way back over to the brick chimney, where he had mounted the control panel. The alarm on his watch told him it was time. He took a deep breath.

Dumb Shit. *That's exactly what the epitaph on my headstone will read. Just those two words. In bold letters.*

"I hope I'm not going to regret this." Alex squeezed his eyes tightly, and opened them again. "Here goes."

Alex thoughtfully went through a series of switches and plugs. He reached to flip the final lever.

In that last split second, he glanced down with a nod, acknowledging a dozen or so members of the city's finest, all dressed in full gear, standing silent, in a curve, giving depth to a circle that didn't actually exist.

Along with them, waiting on the ground were foam tanks and huge hoses, poised high in the air, aimed directly at the house, waiting to be released at full-force.

Frank, Ryan and Danny looked at each other. Emotionally trapped somewhere in between knowing they were in trouble and the excitement and anticipation that this event might work after all, they stood together, like brothers.

Then, like *tipped dominoes*, one-by-one, they looked over at Nick in unison.

And although Nick's expression lacked a smile and he didn't look back at them, they knew their no-nonsense, *tough-guy* leader had made it possible, and insisted on being included.

Alex cringed as he flipped the last switch. His expression matched the sinking sensation in his gut. He started to stand up.

There was an enormous, explosive flash.

As if it was all playing out in slow motion, a simple collective drawn-out phrase resonated from the ground below.

"... Ohhh ... SHIT!!"

And without warning, Alex dropped out of sight.

Everything went black.

~ FORTY-THREE ~

Haunting sirens, wailing in the distance, were rapidly becoming overshadowed by flashing lights gaining intensity in the foreground.

A roadblock of first responders' vehicles skewed across the neighborhood entrance was the first clue that something was very wrong. Strobes blazed everywhere, in blinding shades of red and blue, providing stiff competition for the city lights reflecting off the lake.

That was the second clue.

The untamed energy of a curious crowd, overloaded the night air, making it difficult to breathe. An unattended ambulance waited by the side of the road as frustrated police officers struggled to restrain aggressive, curious onlookers.

Beyond the bend, directly above the homes on the ridge, the night sky glowed with an ominous, eerie radiance.

Headlights rounded the corner, growing larger as a car approached, barely skidding to a stop before the driver's door flew open.

Sarah vaulted from the vehicle, slipping on the icy street as she fought through the crowd, desperately trying to break through the roadblock. She was first ignored, and then held back by the police. She protested, jerking against the unrelenting grip on her arms.

"Please ... *God, Please*! My grandmother's house is up there! Let me through!" Cold wind whistled through the air, chapping her cheeks.

Heartbroken and helpless, tears streaming down her face, Sarah fixed her stare up at the horizon. She gulped, the realization sinking in that her hopes, dreams and memories were most likely being reduced to a mere pile of flickering embers.

Frank, on the other side of the barrier, finally heard, then saw her. He recognized Sarah from the pictures his brother had shown him. She looked a little different than he'd remembered. But he knew it was her. He pushed through the crowd.

"*Sarah?*"

She nodded, waterworks continuing to trickle down her face.

Frank held his hand out to her. "I think you'd better come with me."

Hearing the words, the crowd hushed slightly, looked at her curiously, and slowly parted.

Her heart jumped. Her stomach tightened. Sarah made her way over to the handsome firefighter, who took her shaking hand and rolled his eyes.

"You're *not* going to *believe* this."

The crackling reflection of light reflected off Sarah's face, with more intensity, as she began walking down the street, toward the house. The moment she rounded the bend in the street, her eyes slowly moved from the ground, upward to the house.

~ FORTY-FOUR ~

IT WAS BEYOND BEAUTIFUL. The entire house was completely decked out in Sarah's grandfather's old vintage strings of lights and 1950's decorations.

But that was *impossible*! Because there was no way they could work after all that time and age. But they did. And they were more magnificent than ever.

Sarah stood with her free hand tented over her eyes, gazing at the picture before her. Her hand slipped away from Frank's. She began to wander.

She walked around the front of the house, touching everything she could, as if she didn't think it could be real.

"Exactly twenty three!"

Sarah's eyes moved upward to a figure, shouting down at her from the peak of the roof, next to the beautifully lit star.

It was Alex. Sarah looked up, straining her eyes.

Alex's heart folded over at the sight of her.

"What are you talking about? Twenty three *what*?" she shouted.

The Alex on the rooftop was irresistible with his rough, two day-old shadow-chiseled face. He stretched his arms high in the air, as if to be making a declaration.

*"**Stars**!! Count them! Go on; **I dare you**!!"*

"Alex! What's wrong with you??" Sarah clutched at the hem of her jacket and twisted her scarf. She was on the verge of panic.

She was sure he was either drunk or high on something, even though she knew he didn't indulge in that kind of stuff. Sarah was rattled.

"Come down from there before you kill yourself!" She gulped. "This is *crazy!* How did you *do* all of this?"

A rush of pure adrenaline coursed through him. Alex shouted down at her. "*Awww* ... It takes all of the *fun* out of it if you have to have a reasonable explanation for everything!"

Still on the rooftop, Alex took a running start. Sarah's heart skipped a beat. She shrieked, "*Alex!* Stop! *No!*"

Alex felt almost invincible and full of resolve. He slid down to the second level, his heels finally skidding to a stop, just at the roof's edge. Without hesitation, he leaped to the first level roof and plopped himself down with his legs dangling over the edge.

He grinned down at Sarah, then arched his eyebrows, and shrugged his shoulders.

Then she saw it. His *eyes!* - The *twinkle* was back!

Alex quickly stood again, arms extended, carelessly teetering along the roof's edge, like he was on a balance beam.

Sarah gasped.

Alex spun around on one leg. He stopped suddenly and pointed at her. He backed away, rushing toward the ladder. "Don't go away. I'll be right there."

Alex descended the ladder, skipping the bottom three rungs. He jumped to the ground, and picked up a box from the driveway. He raced over to Sarah's side.

In what felt to Sarah like slow motion, Alex reached around his back to reveal the old cardboard box the man had given him - no wrapping paper. The box was labeled with the barely legible words, faded with time:

LEAVE WITH GMA AND GPA.

There was nothing else on it except a tag, hand-written by Alex, that simply read,

Missed opportunities will find their way back to you, if they are meant to be.

Puzzled, Sarah silently opened the flaps and pulled out the familiar, shiny red treasure box from so long ago.

She lifted the top off the box, and found the big red envelope. Sarah carefully caressed the front of the aged, homemade heart, and then opened it slowly. She ran her fingers along the little bit of red and gold glitter that had stood the test of time. Her lips silently formed the word:

Forever?

Sarah sank to the snow-packed pavement, resting in a sitting position, her legs too shaky to support her.

That day on the playground ... so many years ago - it was all returning to her.

9 year old Sarah notices the boy walking toward her. She smiles at him, leaning around her friend Katie, who is blocking her sight line.

Katie leaves with another girl and the first bell rings. She sees that the boy has something in his hand. She begins walking toward him, but the tardy bell sounds, and he runs away, with his buddies, to line up at the door.

She watches the red envelope fall out from under his jacket.

After he has gone, she quickly, without being noticed, picks it up, sees there's no name on the envelope, and tucks it under her coat.

Back in her classroom coatroom, she discreetly opens the envelope and finds the clumsy, yet wonderful Valentine inside. Smiling, she knows it was meant for her. Her eyes move down to the bottom of the card to see what his name is. It is signed simply, AJ.

Sarah places the card back in its envelope and secures it in the inside pocket of her coat. Hearing the teacher's voice, she scurries out of the coat room to her desk.

Later the same night, Sarah is sitting on her bed, crying as her mother and grandmother break the news to her that her dad has been transferred to New York, and they are moving in just 4 days.

The telephone rings. Her mother leaves the room to answer it. Sarah's grandmother, Irene, feels her pain. She sits next to her, stroking her hair.

"Darling, I know you are upset that you are moving, but you'll make new friends in New York." Putting her arm around her, she continues, "Mom and Dad didn't want to tell you earlier, because they thought you would be more upset. I wish I could have told you sooner."

Irene sighs. Then she smiles sweetly.

"You can come back every Christmas to visit. Your room in our house will always be waiting for you." She walked to the door, and then she turned back to Sarah. "I'll bet we can even talk mom into letting you spend every summer with grandpa and me."

Sarah takes her glasses off, wipes her eyes and sniffles a little. She smiles, half-heartedly, at her grandmother.

"At least I have Monday to say goodbye to all my friends." Irene rushes back over to Sarah and gives her a big hug.

"That's my girl! You'll see. You will love New York!"

"Goodnight, sweetheart," she told her, giving her a kiss on the forehead. Sarah lies down and waits for her grandmother to turn the light off and leave the room.

She reaches under her pillow and pulls out the big red envelope. Springing out of bed, she drops to her knees and reaches below, pulling out a shiny red box.

Not just any box; her secret "treasure box." She lifts off the top, slipping the valentine inside, before quickly closing it again. Sarah slides the box back under the bed.

She climbs back into bed and drifts off to sleep with a smile.

Sunday Night

The voice of the legendary local TV weatherman fades in, talking about the winter weather in Cleveland. Sarah is lying on the floor, watching TV. She is surrounded by dozens of packing boxes, filled, sealed and waiting to be transported to New York.

Sarah sits up quickly, with a look of devastation, as she listens to the weatherman continue.

"Folks, it looks like winter is back, and with a vengeance. You can expect anywhere from 12 to 18 inches of snow by the morning, depending on where you live."

He looks straight at the camera, but it looks like he is addressing Sarah personally.

"I just got the word that should make you kids happy. All schools in Cleveland and the suburbs have called off tomorrow.
Yes, you heard me right. Monday is going to be a "snow day.""

Sarah jumps up, runs down the hall to her room, and slams her door, flinging herself on the bed.

Tears welling in her eyes, she pulls the treasure box out from under the bed, removing the red envelope. She opens it, sniffling. A single tear runs down her cheek as she quickly closes the card and jams it back into the envelope.

Rushing toward the waste basket, Sarah trips over the boxes in her room, each clearly labeled one of two different ways:

TAKE WITH and *LEAVE WITH GMA AND GPA*

Making a conscious decision, Sarah angrily throws the envelope in the trash and turns to leave the room. But she stops, then runs back over and retrieves the big red envelope from the can and places it back in the red box.

Sarah hastily tosses her secret treasure box in a packing box on her way to the door.

~ FORTY-FIVE ~

THE LIGHTLY FALLING SNOW had turned into a thick blanket of white around her. Sarah blinked back to the present as she closed the card. She struggled to understand.

As she glanced up, she recognized the figure of her grandmother, standing in the driveway, wrapped in a firefighter's jacket, being supported by Father McBurney and Nick.

Irene looked exhausted, but very happy. And at peace.

Alex was kneeling next to Sarah in the snow. His eyes carefully examined her face. He stood and pulled her to her feet. Once they were both standing, he drew her closer.

He tilted her face upward and he stroked her cheek with heartbreaking tenderness. Leaning in, Alex gave her a gentle kiss.

Sarah's face glowed. Her eyes slowly closed, lulled by the rhythm of his words. He nervously cleared his throat.

"Hi. I don't believe we were ever properly introduced. My name is *AJ*."

Her body tingled with his words. Awareness registered in her eyes. She held a trembling hand out to him and smiled. "I'm Sarah."

They embraced.

Alex pulled back a little. He stared at her and cupped her face in his hands. Starting out calmly, he gradually progressed into a voice filled with drive and passion - his dark eyes glittering with desire, his features so handsome in the reflection of the lights.

"Sarah, I don't want to spend another Valentine's Day, or Christmas, or 4th of July, or *any* day, for that matter, without you."

"But you don't believe in forever," she whispered.

His gaze sobered. "Forever is composed of a series of nows and thens. And I think we've already covered them both." He reached for her hand. "I never realized it, but you have always been a part of me."

The breeze off the lake picked up and blew through the gathering.

And finally, Sarah wept. "I'm really not crying," she said, wiping her eyes.

Alex touched a tear with his finger. "Yes you are - and it's okay."

He kissed every available inch of Sarah's face. Her bones dissolved. He struggled to push back the vision in his head of stripping off her clothes and making love to her in the snow.

Alex kissed her again, long and sweet, before saying the things he wished he'd said to her long ago.

Sarah and Alex were interrupted by the sound of Frank's voice. He approached them, while on his phone with his wife, Robyn.

Frank paced back and forth in front of the old Cunningham place, apologizing. "Honey, I'm sorry. I promise I'll be home soon; we'll get everything done in time." He glanced at his watch and shook his head. "Don't worry; it will be fine."

Alex and Sarah looked over at Frank. Alex asked, "Is Robyn Okay?

Frank rubbed his chin. "Oh, she's fine. *I'm* the one who's in the doghouse. She's watching this on the news, and I'm supposed to be home, helping her decorate for the party tonight."

He took a deep, helpless breath and continued. "Everybody will be there soon and I'm not even home yet."

"Robyn lives for parties. She's kind of designated herself as our *social director*," Alex explained to Sarah.

"And how she manages to pull off such a great Christmas Eve Party every year in our little house, never ceases to amaze everybody," Frank added.

Sarah and Alex exchanged a knowing look. A smile lit up Sarah's still-damp eyes. She stared over to the big, beautifully decorated, old house and back at Alex.

"I've got an idea ..." She glowed. "Frank - get Robyn back on the phone!"

~ FORTY-SIX ~

The on-duty firefighters gathered around the TV in the common area, watching the local news. Cheers erupted throughout the station as the word spread of what had transpired on that snowy Christmas Eve in northeast Ohio.

Even the national news weighed in on the developing story that was brewing in Cleveland, Ohio. Helicopters circled overhead, eager to be the first to share video footage with the rest of the world.

With bewildered, yet jubilant dismay while delivering the Christmas Eve weather forecast, the legendary local meteorologist romanced the TV camera as live video coverage played out on the screen.

"... and folks ... just as a precautionary measure ... you might want to avoid the Edgecliff area tonight - especially if you want to get somewhere in a timely fashion." He winked at the camera in his familiar, teasing manner.

Images of the Edgecliff neighborhood flashed across television screens. Dozens of delivery vehicles, representing local and chain eateries lined the streets surrounding Edgecliff, causing a major traffic jam, all with the goal of reaching the old Cunningham house with their culinary contributions toward the resurrected, epic Christmas Eve tradition.

History, in its own unique way, was re-creating itself.

"There seems to be an inexplicable phenomenon happening as we are airing tonight." The camera zoomed in on his face, as if it knew the significance of his next words. "All I can tell you for sure is that the spirit of the city appears to be unfolding in front of our very eyes."

Further addressing the camera, with his timeless charismatic smile, he exclaimed,
"It's a great night to be in Cleveland!"

~ FORTY-SEVEN ~

AS THE PARTY WOUND DOWN, Alex walked past the entrance to the living room while talking to a young firefighter with a plate of food, in the doorway leading into the kitchen.

He noticed Sarah, alone, staring out at the Cleveland skyline, from the living room picture window. She was talking on her phone, looking sad.

Excusing himself, he quietly approached Sarah, slipping his arms around her waist from behind. He pulled her against him, as she ended her call. "You look deep in thought."

Sarah turned to him with a weak smile. "I just talked to Mary."

Alex tried to reassure her. "Everything will be OK. It will all work out."

She interrupted him. "Alex - you were right. I *do* need to grow up and start being responsible. It's crazy, but I was *really* thinking I could live here." She took a deep breath.

"I don't know how I could ever take on the financial responsibility of this house. I don't even know if I can get a job that can support *me*; let alone maintaining this house in the way it deserves to be."

Alex gently tried to stop her.

"Sarah - I never meant that you were not responsible. In fact, you are probably more responsible than me in some ways."

Sarah stared out at the Cleveland skyline. "I didn't tell you that the actual reason I came back was because she called me from Colorado to tell me she got a call from a prospective buyer."

Alex seemed mildly surprised at Sarah's news. His eyes crinkled around the edges. "I didn't think the house was on the market yet."

"It wasn't. I didn't really think she could keep it a secret. But," she continued, nervously, "Alex ... her buyer *flat out* offered *10 percent* above the appraised value ... sight-unseen!"

And that's when it hit him.

Sarah had been brave enough to face down her past. It was time for him to do the same - and come clean with what he had done to get her to come back to Cleveland so soon.

Alex reached out and took both of her hands in his. He inhaled a deep breath. "Sarah, you know, I've been thinking ... maybe ..."

She turned away from him. "Alex; I couldn't do it."

He was stunned. "You couldn't do *what*?"

Sarah twirled her hair around her fingers. She looked back at him. "I told Mary the house is not for sale." She sighed.

"She was not happy with me, to say the least. She wasn't looking forward to calling her buyer back tonight with the news."

As Sarah finished the sentence, Alex got a call on his phone. He turned to walk away, excusing himself. "I've got to take this."

Hiding a tiny grin, he spoke into the phone. "Hey, Mary ... *What*?"

He stepped out onto the patio. "What do you mean the house is *not on the market* anymore?"

180

~ FORTY-EIGHT ~

ALEX, UNAWARE THAT SARAH had overheard his phone conversation, and had followed him out onto the patio, turned and was met with her firm grasp on his forearm.

"You didn't."

Alex turned his head. His jaw dropped at the sight of Sarah, spying on him in the moonlight on the patio. He had a quick glimpse of what Sarah looked like as a little girl.

God, she is incredible.

All he wanted to do was throw her on the old, dilapidated snow-covered 1960's picnic table and finish what he had started two nights ago. But this was not the time.

"I did." He winked at Sarah and then he added with a cocky grin, "It was totally brilliant, wasn't it?"

"Or monumentally stupid," Sarah replied with a smirk. "That could have cost you a whole lot of money. That's not like the prudent Alex I have grown to know and love."

Alex cleared off the snow and sat on the old picnic table. He drew Sarah in tight, close to him.

It was as if they were in the middle of a snow globe that had been slightly shaken; finally tranquil and silent.

Sarah felt safe in their little glass jar.

She smelled like flowers and cinnamon. Alex tried desperately to will his body to ignore what was clearly happening.

Not now! Don't pick now to demonstrate how fucking hot you think she is, Wagner. A time and place for everything, asshole.

Sarah plunked herself down next to him on the table.

"Shit, Sarah. I can't explain what's changed ... *in my head.* We were going in completely different directions." He caressed her cheek.

"All I could see was a picture of a storm. I wasted so much time trying to outrun it. And the whole time, you were busy painting a rainbow." He brushed the tiny snowflakes off her hair. "Since you came *crashing* into my life ..."

Sarah eyed him with a little frown.

Alex stood and finished his sentence. " ... I don't worry as much about the little stuff, like I used to." Then with a slightly crooked grin, he added, "Now, that doesn't mean I'm not going to try and stop you if you go off on some *crazy-ass* idea."

Sarah smiled and gave him an affectionate smack on his thigh.

Without a word, he met her gaze and gently grabbed her hand, redirecting it between his legs. Alex's unyielding eyes were doing peculiar things to her. Sarah's heart fluttered wildly at the thought of what he was thinking about.

It was obvious.

Really? Right here?

Sarah ignited, slowly moving in closer and straddled him. She draped her arms around Alex's neck and strained against him as she tried to get as close as she could.

He slipped his hands under her butt and squeezed.

She wrapped her legs around him as he picked her up, heading for the door leading from the patio to the guest room.

Alex fumbled to get the corroded old handle to turn with his one free hand. He couldn't get it open fast enough. But it finally did.

Once inside the warmth of the room, Alex shoved it closed and carried her to the door leading into the hallway. He forcefully kicked it shut. He lowered her onto the bed and pinned her.

Lacing his fingers with Sarah's; a reassurance - not a restraint, he locked on her eyes. Alex released her hands and unfastened her jeans. His hands found the delicate lace bands of her panties.

Sarah shivered. Her face met him with an expression that his body just couldn't ignore any longer.

Alex breathed in deeply, admitting defeat. "I am so screwed."

Sarah whispered back, "You're about to be." A soft smile fell across her lips. "Paint me a rainbow."

~ FORTY-NINE ~

THE PARTY HAD ENDED and just about everybody had gone home or back to work.

Sarah was in the living room; sound asleep on the sofa, in front of the fireplace. There were still a few remnants scattered about the house from the party. The sole source of illumination - the lights and decorations on the Christmas tree, provided a serene aura of magic in the room.

The peaceful quiet of the evening was suspended by conversation coming from the kitchen.

Alex was by the sink, along with Frank, Ryan, Danny and Nick. Alex scraped a plate into a trash bag. He looked up as he tied the bag in the can.

"You guys still here? It's late; go home. It's Christmas - you should be with your families."

Danny smiled. "We'll just help you with the last of this clean-up; it's the least we can do."

Nick grabbed two trash bags and headed to the door with them. Alex turned the lock, opening it and pushed the screen with his knee. Nick turned to Alex.

"Hey, did you say the Bel Aire is still in the garage?"

"Yeah. And it can't look much different than the last time it was driven. Time has been really *kind* to her."

Alex finished tying another bag and added, "We can take a look at her, if you have time, before you leave. And just *wait* until you hear her fire up."

"What a great party. It was almost like I was back there again; I kept waiting for Wink and Irene to come through the door," Ryan added.

Nick and Ryan laughed. The others grabbed the remaining trash bags and headed for the door. They stepped out onto the driveway, at the side of the house, where others were already piled, covered with accumulated snow. They deposited the bags and walked toward the garage.

It was snowing steadily, but there was no wind, making it feel almost warm. Alex walked to the front of the garage, leading the way. He placed his hands on the right side of the huge double-handled door.

"You guys might have to help me get this open. It's manual ... and *heavy*. The springs are probably not in great shape ... so be careful."

They all participated in the challenge, and the bottom edge of the entrance began to separate from the concrete. The door groaned with aging agony, rising slowly. But once it reached the half-way point, it seemed to open by itself. The conversation between the guys stopped in mid-stream.

Alex was dazed. The Bel Aire was not in the garage.

Panic skittered up his spine. "Shit! Did some asshole steal it?"

Nick hastily grabbed a flashlight from the workbench and shined it into the far corners of the garage, as if the massive car could have somehow been hiding in a tiny corner. Frank checked the side of the garage for signs of breaking and entering. He found nothing suspicious.

Danny and Ryan checked around the driveway, looking for fresh tire tracks. Or tracks of any kind.

There were none. Alex raked his fingers across his scalp.

Did somebody take it during that short period of time I went to get Irene?

Nick looked at Alex; Danny looked at Frank and Ryan. Collectively, they stood, frozen and stared into the space the Bel Aire had occupied.

Any woman, regardless of her age, would have been delighted at the rear-view vision of these five, physically fit men in a row, staring into the empty garage, if it hadn't been for the fact that it wasn't for a good reason.

They were perplexed - befuddled and stupefied.

Their shared silhouette became more pronounced, as bouncing dots of light gradually appeared on the horizon behind them.

It wasn't the moonlight. And it wasn't from the lamp posts on the street.

A set of headlights was slowly turning onto Edgecliff Drive. Increasing in size, the beam looked a lot like spotlights. The five guys turned to face the street and stared without a word, as they watched a car approach. Their mouths dropped open.

"What the shit?!"

A red, two-tone 1955 Chevy Bel Aire pulled up to the curb. It stopped, idling, with the headlights still on, windshield wipers rhythmically wiping the falling snow off the windshield.

The car was covered in snow, yet it looked brand new. They walked down the driveway, together.

Just as they reached the curb, the driver's side door opened and a figure stepped out. It was hard to see much detail at first, through the snow, but they could see that it was a man, in his late 20's, dressed in a uniform.

Walking into the beam from the headlights, the man stopped just short of the curb. He appeared to be a firefighter; a Lieutenant, in dress uniform, from the 1950's.

Speechless, and a little spooked, the five listened as the man addressed them. "I just had to stop by to see the place." He looked up at the peak of the roof and the patched-together star, and he smiled.

"It's all about *vision, faith and memories*. And what you *do* with them, isn't it?

Alex noticed, for the first time, that the star was completely lit up, even though it was not plugged into an electrical outlet. The cord dangled in the breeze from the lake. The hair on the back of Alex's neck stood on end, as he grabbed Frank's arm. Frank's eyes widened as he looked up too.

The young Lieutenant then turned and addressed them all.

"We each have many memories in our lifetime to pick from. It's up to you to choose the very best ones, and keep them with you always, for safekeeping."

The guys inched a little closer, but stopped when the lake breeze and snow picked up, circling the car and the man.

The cloud settled. They found themselves standing in front of a different firefighter; a Chief in his late sixties, in full dress uniform from the 1990's. Alex recognized him immediately as the man who helped him get the old house decked out. He smiled.

It was Wink.

Chief Winston Cunningham addressed them. *"There is more than one side to every story."* He took a breath, looking downward momentarily, then he centered back on Nick.

Nick, I know you can't forget that night; *nothing* can change that." He paused. "But when you *do* remember that night, instead of thinking about what happened to *me*, I want you to think about what *could have happened*, if you *hadn't* gone back in when you did.

Nick took a step toward the man. *"**But** ..."*

Wink held his hand up to silence him. "Nick - it was *my time*. Do you understand me?"

Nick searched his eyes, studying the man he'd idolized, so many years ago. "I think so."

Wink turned. He stepped over to the open car door and leaned to get back into the driver's seat. He hesitated, and then he backed out, as if he had forgotten something. Ryan walked toward Wink, but Nick put his hand on his shoulder, gently holding him back.

Wink took a step toward Alex. *"Hey, son!"* He reached into his coat pocket and pulled something out, tossing it in Alex's direction.

"Take good care of these."

Alex reached up with both hands, to catch it. A set of 5 keys on a chain, attached to a little fob depicting an emblem representing the city fire department flew through the air, in slow motion, toward Alex.

He caught them with a smile.

"You bet I will!"

And, with Alex's *catch of the keys*, the young Lieutenant from the 1950's returned in the older man's place. He nodded at Alex and the others and gestured to them.

They could each feel the burn of joy building in their eyes as they sensed that the encounter with Wink was drawing to a close. They waved back.

He smiled again at them, cocking his cover slightly forward, with a nod. "Make it a good one." And with that, Lieutenant Cunningham got into the car and shifted it into gear.

As the car slowly passed the driveway, the passenger window came down a little - just enough to see the pretty 25 year-old Irene smile and wave at them. The window went back up as the car pulled slowly down the street, making the turn off Edgecliff Drive.

The head and taillights got smaller, eventually fading into a glittery mist sweeping off toward the Cleveland skyline as the five watched in awe. The lights appeared to settle over the far-right point.

They disappeared completely - then, a point of light on the skyline shimmered.

And out of the blue … it *winked*.

~ A FEW DAYS LATER ~

EPILOGUE

THE SUN HAD REACHED its peak and was already making its way back down, looping through the late afternoon sky. But the air was still warm for winter and rich with the sweet fragrance of life.

Alex, Frank, Ryan, Danny and Nick, handsomely dressed in business attire and winter coats, walked together along the sidewalk on the snow-covered ridge by the park. They stopped and looked out over the metropolitan view of downtown Cleveland.

Nick picked up a flat stone and quickly leaned back, hurling it in a parallel direction. It skipped four times before finding its final resting place in Lake Erie.

"What a nice memorial. I couldn't believe how many people were there. There had to be at least two hundred people crammed into that little chapel."

Ryan added, "Father McBurney did a real good job with the service, didn't he?"

Danny smiled and sighed, "You know, I'm a little jealous. I really wish I had known Irene ... *and* Wink. They must have been some nice people."

Frank put his arm across the back of Alex's shoulders. "Alex - I don't think you will ever know how much I admire you - and what you have done ... *for everybody.*"

Alex smiled appreciatively as he gestured toward the sky over the lake, listening to the water lap at the shore. "I wish there was something else we could do."

Curious, they looked at him.

Alex smiled and explained, "You know ... some little way for *us* to pay a tribute to both Irene *and* Wink."

Frank nodded with a smile. "Yeah; especially since we're the only ones who saw what we saw ... and know what we know."

Danny unbuttoned the top button of his coat. "I know I can *never* tell *anybody* about what happened. I'd be sent for a psychiatric evaluation."

They were still laughing as a figure, in a dark topcoat, appeared on the horizon, becoming greater as it drew near.

Father McBurney approached.

Nick held his grip steadfast on father's hand, as they found themselves eye-to-eye. "Thank you for everything, father. I know both Irene and Wink would have been humbled by your kind words."

Father McBurney's lips turned slightly upward at the implied compliment. "Oh, I didn't say anything that wasn't the absolute truth. *They* did the *important* part." He pivoted into the cooling breeze off the lake as he put his gloves on, and added, "We'd better head back. I was sent out here to fetch you back to the house. It's about time for dinner."

Together they walked in the direction of the house, without conversation.

Suddenly, without giving it any thought, Alex reached down and grabbed a handful of snow, creating a huge ball. He turned quickly and set his aim as if there was a giant bulls-eye on Frank's back. He grinned and shouted,

"Hey, Frank!"

Frank was no fool, possessing a unique combination of having graduated at the top of his class in *Snowball Fighting* and his inherited *lightning-fast reflexes*. He instinctively ducked.

And the snowball flew right over him.

An eerie silence followed.

Coming from the direction the snowball had set off in, came a voice, increasing in volume as it inched closer and closer.

The guys were quickly beginning to get the feeling that perhaps they weren't the only ones that afternoon, out there on the ridge along Lake Erie.

They turned slowly, only to find themselves being approached by an older woman, in her late 80's. She was holding Alex's rogue snowball in her hand.

And she appeared to be quite unhappy.

She marched over, getting right in Alex's face, holding the snowball up to his nose. Her intense green eyes locked on his.

Alex's mouth dropped open. He was frozen, somewhere in between astonishment and fear.

"Are you responsible for this?"

Shit!

He had gotten himself into more trouble in the last month than he had in his entire 32 years of life. His answer sounded like something between a defense and an apology.

"No, ma'am. Not me."

She shot a narrow-eyed look and snapped at him. "You lie as bad as you throw." She gripped him by the shoulder, her narrow fingers surprisingly strong.

Then, jabbing her index finger at him, she continued to drive her point home. *"You know ... you could have hit me with this."* Following with more intensity, *"You know, I haven't lost my temper in 40 years. But Sonny ... you could have really hurt somebody!"*

Repeatedly smacking the ball against Alex's chest, she added,

"Somebody 'oughta belt you with this thing."

Alex backed up, but the woman stepped closer to him. He felt a lump descend to the bottom of his stomach. With each sentence, she whacked the solid little mound of snow harder against his chest.

"But I won't ... I won't."

She finally turned away, taking a couple steps to depart.

Alex sighed in relief. *Thank God. I thought she would **never** leave.*

But in a surprise move, the woman suddenly spun back to him, sporting an unmistakable, impish grin.

*"... **The HELL I won't!**"* She threw the snowball hard, aiming straight at Alex.

But Alex had inherited the family *quick-reflex gene* as well.

He dropped to the bank of snow, losing his balance, just as the ball whizzed past him, grazing his right temple. He blinked in response to the strength of the woman's pitching ability.

Everybody on the ridge froze as they watched the snowball, in slow motion, smack Father McBurney, who had just put his hands in his pockets, square in the side of the head.

The feisty, silver-haired senior covered her eyes with her hands as the realization set in that she had just hit a priest in the head with her snowball. Her mouth dropped open.

She was mortified. And speechless.

The ridge was completely silent as everyone waited to see if the father was alright.

Standing high on the mound across the ridge, a stunned Father McBurney turned to establish the identity of his assailant. He tilted his head back, to the heavens above.

"Aw ... come on now! You know ... just a little bit of divine intervention wouldn't hurt ... once in awhile; would it?"

He shook his head and knelt down on the mound, expressionless. Was he praying?

A tangle of arms and legs tore across the ridge to make sure he hadn't been injured by the old lady's snowball missile. Frank and Nick already had their phones out, calling EMS to the scene.

But as they approached him, Father McBurney grinned and reached down into the snowdrift. He packed a hefty-sized snowball. Everybody automatically backed away from him.

Father hesitated for a moment. Collectively, they held one giant breath. He quickly glanced upward again and made the sign of the cross, still holding the tightly packed ball in his hand.

Without warning, Father McBurney stood, winding up for the pitch and proclaimed,

"Every man for himself!"

He fast-pitched the snowball, sending it westward into the afternoon sky. Bursting with pride, he turned as he shouted and bragged,

"I always wanted to play in the *Major Leagues*!"

But his grin promptly faded with the sound of a thud - not a particularly loud one. But a *thud,* nonetheless.

They all turned, hands cupped over their eyes, squinting into the setting sun. Father McBurney could only make out the distinct silhouette of a man dusting off his butt. Then the man leaned over to pick up what he could only assume was the ball he had just sent across the ridge.

When he had made the pitch, the ball had seemed so much larger than it was looking now. The figure continued walking slowly in his direction.

The old lady leaned into Father McBurney and handed him her rosary. "Here. Judging by the looks of this, I think you're going to need this more than I will."

The outline of the man continued to increase in size as he got closer. And then, just when they were hoping the silhouette wouldn't get any larger, it didn't. A sigh of relief echoed across the ridge.

But what they hadn't noticed was that, while he stopped getting *bigger*, the man continued to get *taller* with every step closer to them.

The sun, perhaps also a little worried, hid briefly behind a purple cloud. But that only made it easier to identify who Father McBurney had just assaulted. The man approached the mound and stopped in front of him. The logo on his wine and gold jacket was unmistakable.

He held up the snowball. And that's when they all began to sweat what Father McBurney had done.

Had he delivered a fast-pitch to the buttocks of one of the *Cleveland Cavaliers*?

Everybody gasped. They waited to see what the man had in store for Father McBurney.

He looked down at father and said, "You know, if I threw a ball like that I sure as *hell* wouldn't be bragging about it." He glanced upward, apologetically, and corrected himself. "I meant sure as *shit*."

Yeah, like *that* was better.

All activity suspended; the silence was deafening. His expression softened as he put the ball down and knelt on the mound, scooping fresh snow into his hands.

They all watched silently, in awe, as the man began fashioning his own snowball. He packed the wet snow tightly and lectured him.

"You're going about it *all wrong*."

He began rolling the ball he had just packed in another layer of wet snow. And then more layers; until he had rolled a snowball, *ginormous in size*, just under nine and a half inches in diameter. He continued,

"Now, *this* is a ball. This is the secret ... *this* is what gives it its momentum."

He stood and handed the ball to Father McBurney. "Try it now."

But Father McBurney was hesitant to take it. The hefty snowball slipped through his hands, tumbling to the ground, partly because he didn't want to make the mistake of hitting another innocent bystander, partly because it was heavy, but mostly because he was *just plain intimidated*.

The man rolled his eyes and exhaled hard. "Do I have to show you how to do *everything*?" He assumed the position on the mound. He jumped and lunged forward, releasing the ball.

All heads turned upward, following it as it sailed toward the lake and disappeared over the ridge to the beach.

He displayed a cocky grin. "See? Now, *that's* how you do it."

However, the training session was rudely interrupted by a yet different voice, booming from beyond.

"What the hell is this?"

Everybody turned to the direction the voice was coming from but the scene was void of human life. Among footsteps crunching through the snow, they heard more cursing. And it was getting louder and louder.

The monster snowball made an awkward encore appearance on the ridge. It was immediately followed by a head, appearing from the lip separating the beach from the ridge.

The reflections from the setting sun made it temporarily difficult to distinguish the identity of the head and the man attached to it. He continued the climb over the lip.

Another jacket with a logo; brown accented with orange that spelled out *The Cleveland Browns*.

This man was breathing heavily, carrying the previous man's weighty snowball. "I'll show you how to do this ... *the right way!"*

He placed the massive ball of snow on the ground in front of him and pulled out a pocket knife. Everybody gulped and backed away.

The man looked over at them and snickered, waving the knife. "What a bunch of *wimps*."

He jabbed the knife into one side of the ball and carved out a concave curve. Then he pivoted the ball and repeated the procedure on the opposite side. He smoothed and polished the entire surface with his gloved hands, crafting the two ends into dull points, until the ball appeared virtually seamless.

Obviously pleased with his creation, the man stood. Arm poised high in the air; he bent his elbow, pulling backward, a mere second away from propelling his snow-marvel high into the heavens over Cleveland.

But a heavy hand grabbed his arm, pulling it and the ball back before it could be released.

The spectators on the ridge snapped their heads sharply to the right as they witnessed the oversized ball being swiped into the hands of another man, wearing yet a *different* jacket. Navy blue with red and white lettering.

The Cleveland Indians.

"I'll take this!" he declared.

The man shook his head as he studied the large, odd-shaped ball. He knelt on the mound and carefully smacked it, causing the outer layers of snow to peel away.

Once he had the general, smaller size he was aiming for, he packed the ball tightly between his hands and recovered its original globular shape.

Sirens filled the air, screaming in the distance, warning that EMS was fast approaching, flanked by the City Police Department.

A crowd was beginning to accumulate on the ridge and along the lakeshore of the beach. Things were beginning to take on the appearance of a standoff.

Like something out of an old movie.

Our side against their side ... and all the other sides.

Then, high on the mound, the man in the Cleveland Indians jacket drew back for the pitch and, with a big grin, exclaimed,

"Free-for-all!!"

Everybody at the scene joined in, scraping together as much snow as possible, flinging it at *anything or anybody* within range. It all happened so fast.

The city safety forces, originally called to the scene to respond to the possibility of a *fallen priest*, sped into the parking lot, nearly taking out the trash cans as their vehicles rushed in.

The first responders found themselves caught up in the moment and joined in, compelled to defend the honor of their *comrades*, taking *the fall* for them, *when and if* necessary.

And it was necessary - *often*.

Park Rangers, one-by-one, on horseback, began to appear, galloping in and dismounting, before enlisting in the forces.

Consisting of teams that had all the earmarks of being assembled by *Goodwill*, a contest of mass confusion followed.

Alex watched from the sidelines as a grin fell across his face. He got it - His measly little snowball had triggered a similar, wacky, *Cleveland snowball-fight* version of the mud-slinging scene from the old John Wayne movie.

A few wispy clouds marred the winter afternoon sky above. It was *downhill* from there.

Literally.

Packed snow, compressed in all shapes and sizes, zigzagged across the late afternoon horizon on the ridge, taking turns knocking the *snow-warriors* off balance, sending them careening down the slippery slope to Edgewater Beach.

Alex's oblivious state of euphoria was interrupted by a hit from a slush missile to the back of the head originating from the east, sending him sailing down the decline, head-first; destination … *Edgewater Beach … ETA – 10 seconds.*

Upon his arrival in the snow pit, a gloved hand reached out to assist Alex to his feet. It was Father McBurney.

"Thanks."

"Don't mention it. Stick with me, kid." He led Alex back up the steep slope, successfully avoiding the *snow-fire*, reaching the crest of the ridge. He turned to Alex with a cocky grin.

"Did I mention I was great at dodgeball back in the third grade?"

Somehow that fact didn't instill Alex with much confidence in him.

With a big grin, he continued, "I've got this. It's in the bag."

But at that very instant, Danny ducked to avoid a shot to his left ribcage, flailing his arms about, losing his stability. He knocked Father McBurney off-balance, plummeting him back down to the bowels of the frozen cavity of Edgewater Beach.

Father staggered to his feet and, once again, dragged himself back up to the ridge. He shielded his eyes with his gloves.

The sun peeked out from behind the deepening clouds just long enough for him to make out the distinct form of more figures, poised to send more snowballs, if necessary.

Just at the moment Father McBurney hunched his shoulders, bracing himself to take a multiple hit, the five on the ridge each took a hit themselves from opposite directions, sending them all flying downward into the snow trench.

Alex dove into a drift of snow, successfully avoiding the impending visit of another snow projectile.

Back up on the ridge, Frank shifted his feet, quite pleased for the temporary reprieve. He took in a deep breath of relief and was about to breathe out.

But not before he was hit by a speedy shot of snow, burning through the chill of the afternoon that could have easily melted the drift beside him.

The snowflakes were getting larger and heavier as the sun continued its decline into the horizon.

Was it shaping up to be a blizzard?

Who could tell? Nobody knew anything for sure.

Nick and Ryan, perched high upon the crest, arms folded, overlooked the beach to assess the situation.

Ryan was suddenly knocked back all of five feet, onto his ass, joining three members of the City Safety Forces team, sliding past him, on their own way down to the pit.

Once at the bottom, dazed, Ryan was pulled to his feet by the man in the Cavs jacket. But the moment he left Ryan, they were both distracted by a shadowy figure careening down the slope in his direction.

"Incoming!!"

They dove into snowdrifts at opposite ends, in self-defense, as the old lady skidded to a stop at the bottom of the hill.

Standing, very proud of her maneuvering skills, she curtsied.

But not for long.

Nick tackled her, from the right, in an instinctive attempt to protect her from the impending barrage of ammunition heading in her direction. He landed on top of her.

Damn that training manual.

"Sorry, ma'am. Are you alright?"

She looked up at Nick and batted her eyes.

"Do Paramedics know how to do mouth-to-mouth?"

Embarrassed, Nick looked down at the woman under him.

"I'm the Fire Chief, ma'am."

The mischievous matron smiled up at him, squeezing his bulging biceps, with a rascally grin.

*"Oohh ... the **Chief**!"*

Nick swiftly jumped up and headed back uphill, to the top of the ridge, joining Frank and Danny.

In the meantime, the remainder of the city firefighters were fighting their own battle.

In theory, they were trained with several stages in mind:

1. *Get in quick.*
2. *Find survivors.*
3. *Get the hell out.*

The situation was not fitting the profile at all.

At the crest of the ridge, a man stood alone, arms crossed as he stiffly surveyed the action. Bearing a striking resemblance to the stereotypical profile of a stodgy 1940's college professor, stuck in a time-warp, he shook his head as Danny approached him.

"You know, this is absurd. These are grown men. I have degrees in Psychology and Sociology. I know everything there is to know about human behavior."

"This couldn't be more fascinating."

Danny rolled his eyes and leaned backward to catch a fly ball off to the left of the man, preventing him from taking a hit to the shoulder. The man didn't flinch. Danny however, suffered multiple shots to his back.

The man just continued talking. Mostly about things that Danny didn't understand.

Nor did he have any desire to.

Again, taking a defensive nosedive in front of the man, Danny deflected another rocket of snow. Unable to successfully secure himself, he rolled uncontrollably down the hill, taking out two others who had been struggling to climb back up to the ridge.

From the opposite side of the rim, the men in the *Browns*, *Cavs* and *Indians* jackets observed the interaction between Danny and the man. Together they moved toward the man and stopped next to him, watching the action.

He hadn't even noticed that the young firefighter had been replaced.

"It has all the earmarks of a testosterone-based, male-bonding … game of some kind. It may as well be a late nineteenth century bar room brawl. "

"Such a *barbaric* ritual." He unfolded his arms. "Fascinating. I don't believe this is covered in my books."

The grinning man in the Browns jacket shouted as the three men ducked simultaneously, giving permission to three incoming snowballs to accomplish what the previous ones should have.

"I'll bet *this* isn't either."

The man lost his balance, careening down the hill in a tailspin, gathering momentum and more casualties along the way to the Edgewater Beach battleground.

Once at the bottom, the man stood, blinded by snow packed tightly in between his face and the lenses of his glasses. He spun in a circle, tripping blindly over two park rangers as they too, attempted to become vertical.

He began the steep climb back to the ridge, stepping over Father McBurney and the others who had joined him on his way down into the bottom of the giant Edgewater snow cone.

High on the ridge, the three men in the jackets smiled and nodded, high-fiving themselves on a job well done. But the moment they turned around to leave, one of them slipped, wavering to keep his balance and remain in a vertical position.

There is something so disturbingly hysterical about seeing an acquaintance take a harmless, frozen slapstick tumble on a late winter afternoon in Cleveland.

And this was no exception.

The other two men giggled; then they laughed uncontrollably as they watched their buddy struggle to regain his balance.

And he did - But not before waging his own war.

Reaching out in a smiling, spirited gesture, he sent the unsuspecting duo speeding down the tightly packed one-way avenue.

The warm afternoon was morphing into a frigid evening, and the Cleveland horizon was blushing into a breathtaking kaleidoscope of color.

You have to be tough to be from Cleveland, but even Clevelanders know when it's time to start thinking about a retreat. The scrap between the dozens of warriors continued, but the velocity was waning.

As if to be issuing a warning, the sun suddenly dipped behind a thick gray cloud.

The shrill shriek of a human taxi whistle cut through the lakefront atmosphere.

"Hey!" The voice paused for only a moment before continuing. *"Cease!* **Immediately!"**

All heads snapped to the mound at the crest of the ridge. As the voice continued, the sun emerged one last time, for an encore performance, to shine a spotlight on the newest cast member.

It was frigid-cold out there on Edgewater Beach, but suddenly there was more sweat present than at a *4ᵗʰ of July* picnic.

The mayor of the city appeared, perched high atop the ridge. He scolded, *"Where are your heads?"* He placed his hands on his hips.

They quietly looked down at the snow-covered ridge beneath their boots.

He went on. "The media outlets are on their way as I speak! Is *this* what you would like to see on the national news? Is *this* how you want our city to be represented all over the world?"

They stared up at the man, in silence – expressionless.

"What do you think they will all be *saying* about us?"

Voices in hushed tones began wafting upward, while heads at the bottom of the ridge leaned together, smiling and nodding in a conspiratorial manner.

" ... *Now* ... I am asking you all to *drag* yourselves back up here, start behaving like adults - *go* home and *back* to work. *Come on now - show the world what we're made of!"*

There was a split moment of deafening silence.

Suddenly, the mayor ducked out of sight, as a spray of at least a dozen snowballs suddenly appeared on the horizon - all originating from Edgewater Beach.

And they were all heading straight for the crest of the ridge.

IRENE'S SUGAR COOKIES

INGREDIENTS:

1 1/2 cups butter, softened
2 cups white sugar
4 eggs
1 teaspoon vanilla extract

5 cups all-purpose flour
2 teaspoons baking powder
1 teaspoon salt

DIRECTIONS:

In a large bowl, cream together butter and sugar until smooth. Beat in eggs and vanilla. Stir in the flour, baking powder, and salt. Cover, and chill dough for at least one hour (or overnight).

Preheat oven to 400 degrees F. Roll out dough on floured surface 1/4 inch thick. Cut into shapes with holiday cookie cutters. Place cookies 1/2 inch apart on ungreased cookie sheets.

Bake 5 to 8 minutes in preheated oven. Cool completely before icing.

JESS'S BLIZZARD BLITZ ICING

INGREDIENTS:

1 stick butter, softened
¼ tsp. salt
2-4 tbsp. cream or milk
½ tsp. vanilla extract

½ tsp. almond extract
2 cups powdered sugar
New Zealand Pino Noir
(optional)*

DIRECTIONS:

Mix together your softened butter, salt, 2 tablespoons of milk, vanilla and almond flavorings.

Adjust the amount of powdered sugar you use according to your preference of consistency. Begin with mixing in 1/2 cup powdered sugar, slowly stirring in more by ¼ cup increments, until the desired consistency is achieved.

If the icing becomes too stiff, add another tablespoon or so of cream or milk.

*If desired, pour 4 ounces of Pino Noir into a glass and enjoy.

FATHER MCBURNEY'S FAMOUS HOLIDAY PUNCH

INGREDIENTS:

1-2 pints Vanilla ice cream

1/8 teaspoon ground cinnamon

8 cups fresh dairy eggnog, chilled

1 small bottle cream soda,
    chilled*

Peppermint/cinnamon sticks or
candy canes (optional)

DIRECTIONS:

Place ice cream in a large punch bowl. Add half the eggnog. Stir and mash mixture using a potato masher until ice cream is melted and mixture is well combined. Stir in remaining eggnog. Slowly pour in cream soda, stirring to combine.

To garnish, add a peppermint or cinnamon stick to each glass.
Or you may prefer to use a candy cane, keeping the festive theme.

Sprinkle lightly with cinnamon (about 1/8 teaspoon per serving).

Makes about 24 (6-ounce) servings.

*... *at your own risk* ... Father McBurney has been known to
  add Irish Cream liquor, to taste, in place of cream soda ...

WINK'S FIREHOUSE 5-ALARM CHILI*

12 quart heavy stock pot

Onion – 1 large, chopped
Ground Chuck 2-3 lbs.
Salt and pepper - to taste
Kidney beans, dark red - 3 cans
Black beans - 2 cans
Green chilies - 1 can, chopped
Green bell peppers - 2, coarsely chopped
Red bell peppers - 2, coarsely chopped
Jalapeños – 2, finely chopped
Habaneros – 1, minced finely
Tomato paste – 2 cans
Diced tomatoes – 1 can (12 oz.)
Crushed tomatoes – 1 can (12 oz.)
Favorite Amber beer – 2 bottles
Minced garlic - 2 heaping tbsps.
Chili powder - 5 tbsps.
Cumin - 2 tbsps.
Crushed red pepper - 2 tsp.
Sugar - 1 tbsp.

Brown meat with onion until onion is transparent. Salt and pepper to taste.

Stir in remaining ingredients except the spices and beer.
Cover and cook down, simmering for about 20-30 minutes, depending on how thick you want the chili to be. Be sure to stir occasionally to keep the mixture from sticking to the bottom of the pot.

Reduce heat. Add beer and spices to taste. Let simmer another 20-30 minutes.

To make 5-Alarm Version: Add 2 more Habaneros, or 1 ghost pepper, if you dare. Put the fire out with sour cream and shredded cheddar cheese.

Motion Picture quotes reference/credit Pg. 164:
"McLintock!. Dir. Andrew V. McLaglen. Perf. John Wayne,
Maureen O'Hara. Paramount Pictures, 1963."